Puppet's Banquet

Valkyrie Loughcrewe

from a story by Daniel Rooney &
Valkyrie Loughcrewe

Cover Art by Donna A. Black
Interior Illustrations by Trevor Henderson
Edited by Alex Woodroe

Content warnings are available at the end of this book. Please consult
this list for any particular subject matter you may be sensitive to.

Selected Works from Tenebrous Press:

Crom Cruach
a novel-in-verse by Valkyrie Loughcrewe

Casual
a novel by Koji A. Dae

All Your Friends are Here
stories by M.Shaw

TRVE CVLT
a novel by Michael Bettendorf

A Spectre is Haunting Greentree
a novel by Carson Winter

One Hand to Hold, One Hand to Carve
a novella by M.Shaw

From the Belly
a novel by Emmett Nahil

Posthaste Manor
a novel by Jolie Toomajan & Carson Winter

The Black Lord
a novella by Colin Hinckley

Dehiscent
a novella by Ashley Deng

Agony's Lodestone
a novella by Laura Keating

Soft Targets
a novella by Carson Winter

Lure
a novella by Tim McGregor

More titles at www.TenebrousPress.com

"Sub-Ornament Creaking Carcasses
Stagger Blackest Harbours
Moored Frothing Profuse"

—Portal,
"Werships"

"I'm coming home, I'm home, I'm coming home"
—Axis of Perdition,
"Heaving Salvation in the Paradise of Rust"

There we are, coming back into the flesh.
Were you dreaming?
Still a bit groggy. That's ok.
No, don't try to speak, you might damage your tongue
Against the wire gauze, in your numbed state.
Follow the light. That's it.
That's it.
It is a very special thing to have you here
for you to be part of this procedure.
Unfortunately, however we—or you, rather, do not
have a lot of time before you begin to . . .
Well,
Let's try and keep things pleasant for now.
I see you're shifting a little in your bonds,
I do hope the restraints aren't too tight.
Toxic shock would really interfere with what we've come to do here
today.
I'm going to put something up on the screen now and I want you
to focus,
focus on the image, and the sound of my voice.
Some of it will be pre-recorded,
the rest of it will be alive,
in here with you.
With us.
And hopefully, once this ends,
you and I will finally understand
why all of this had to happen.

Slide 1:
Verminations in the carrion infinity

Humans were meant to exist in living tribes,
gathered around the fire, bustling nonstop
from sunrise through sunset and beyond
children were meant to sleep to the sound of
crackling fires, murmuring conversation
the tapping of drums and the flutters of music
memory is a network of nodes reaching out to
one another, connecting through story and song
when humans are separated, sorted into right-angled
living catacombs, a kind of decay that sets in
a decay of meaning
and memory
can you imagine the kind of things that
certain people might
get up to?
in their desperation
in search of a signal through the noise?

First, we must draw our attention back to a large, well-kept house nestled in the misty veils of the Irish countryside, as the last clink of cheap porcelain on a tray of expensive silver signalled the end of the evening.

It was followed by an exaggeratedly satisfied sigh, and an equally exaggerated rubbing of hands. It was not taken as obnoxious or unnecessary by the guests. The party had started at twelve in the day and it was approaching eight in the evening. The drinkers were drunk, the drivers were tired, and the gossip had long run dry.

Valkyrie Loughcrewe

Celia and Martin needed no excuse to be the first to filter out, though they did wait for a couple of the older family members to make their way out across the misty gravel driveway to their cars before they followed suit. They didn't want to be rude, and it wasn't as if they didn't get on with Martin's family, or his Uncle Paudy, whose birthday they had been celebrating.

There was, however, a kind of underlying tension to any sort of family gathering, on either side. They were from wealthy stock, our husband and wife, families with ties to heavy industry, real estate, pharmaceuticals, agribusiness and communications, ties to the twin dominant political parties which had robbed the countries blind for decades.

So where did the discomfort come from? Were dear Martin and delicate Celia, beneath it all, revolutionary socialists in the time-honored tradition of their ancestors, aghast at the rape of their beloved green isle? Of course not, the truth was far more banal—the pair had fallen on hard times, their mortgage getting out from under them. Their meagre jobs—Celia a schoolteacher, Martin a middle manager in a floundering infrastructure startup—were not quite cutting through the rolling waves of debt.

Being good Irish Catholics the pair of them, naturally they refused any offers of nepotism, plenary or partial, and by the point of the evening of Paudy Fitzmaurice's seventy sixth birthday, the family had accepted their honourable stubbornness.

For the most part.

"Do you not think maybe you could take yer man a little more seriously?" Celia said, in a small voice as the car door shut behind her.

"Who now?" Martin asked, checking the rear-view mirror of his SUV to make sure there were no children standing behind it for him to reverse over.

For what it's worth, if there had been, he wouldn't have seen them.

"Sean's brother—what was his name?"

"Hannon. Bit of an odd name." Martin sniffed.

"It's a good job he was offering. You're well cut out for it."

"He'll have me doing nothing. Same as me father, sitting at a desk doing piss all while I rake in cash, it's no way to live. I'd turn into a fat-berg and then shrivel up."

Martin chuckled to himself as they pulled out of the driveway, heading down the country lane. The light was failing, the sunset lost to wispy layers of cloud, all stacked on top of each other, such as the otherwise gorgeous view from the Fitzmaurice house was lost to the darkening grey haze.

"A fat-berg?" Celia asked, sounding perturbed.

"Ah, you don't want to know what that is, you'd be put off your dinner, sorry I said it."

Celia would be put off making Martin's dinner, more like. Inside her pale and pretty head, Celia weighed if she should wade into the thorny issue of the futility of Martin's employment. She knew that eventually when the pay dried up completely, he would move on to something better, but his stubbornness, his insistence that the firm was going to have some kind of breakthrough success that would wipe their slate of debt clean, was a menace.

Said debt was always ticking up, as far as Celia was concerned, Martin's machismo was not only prolonging their suffering, but inflaming it. As far as Martin was concerned, the worse things seemed like they were about to get, the more satisfying it would be when the dam broke.

It would be damn near orgasmic, a hand delivered climax to his righteous suffering, eased into being by way of his diligent practice of prayer and Sunday worship. His faith was unshakable, unlike his wife's confidence in her own assertions.

All this aside, to call their marriage unhappy would be disingenuous. Life can't be measured in pennies and pounds, and the pair were known to make each other laugh on occasion. They still enjoyed the warmth of each other's bodies as they drifted off to sleep at night, and their fruitless attempts at fertility were for the most part adequately pleasant experiences.

They were used to the deep, rich vein of discomfort and anxiety in their relationship. Its amniotic fluid carried them, floating, together, from day to languid day.

It is what it is
Driving through the countryside, from lane-vein to road-artery,
to town-organ, barely conscious of the routes
patterns traced like the fingers of God
grooves in the vinyl

Valkyrie Loughcrewe

wrinkles in the brain
in waking sleep
until some external stimulus comes along
to

There is a featureless field, along an uninteresting road, through an uninteresting stretch in the countryside. The odd ivy-choked tree, decaying fenceposts being pulled into the earth by relentless vegetations. Rusted barbwire and unreliable electric wire.

And gates, almost always closed, aside from when the local farmer, all crotchety gait and gaunt, tanned-pink skin, herds his local cows from place to place; always signposted by bright orange traffic cones, flimsy rope barriers. Always in the daylight.

That night, a gate was open along the road, one that Martin did not expect. Darkness had long since fallen as they passed it, not far from the home-stretch, a cosy evening ahead of them of microwave mini pizzas and a glass of wine before bed.

In the split second before the car drifted by the open gate, the driver in his comfortable state of road hypnosis, a pale figure came flailing out of the blackness.

Just a flash of white and the impression of a figure,
the brain having barely a split second to alert the body
fragmentary instant of sheer abject rejection
and the first collision, barely a thump,
she went up and over,
to the second collision
the one against the windshield
turning the clear vision of the road
into a scatteredscrunch of bloody material
tumble tumble across the roof
to the third collision
flesh on tarmac
skin shredded and bones mangled
a body he didn't need
for what was to follow

Their screams were the kind of hysterical shrieks of panic you never hear in movies, the kind of animal sound that can't be faked. You probably would never hear such a sound in your life, unless you happen to be in the vicinity of a car accident, or disturb a dreamer in the midst of a nightmare.

Martin opened his door first, as he found himself beginning to projectile vomit on the dashboard, and figured such emissions were better suited for the tarmac. It wasn't a conscious choice, he was still in shock, but his manners were impeccable, it must be said.

Celia, ever the dutiful wife, followed suit, hearing the click and the hydraulic swing of the door.

She gasped in the night air, seeing only the very edges of the plant-life at the edge of the road, picked up by the very outer limits of the SUV's headlights. Milky-pale, jagged leaves, the impression of a rotted fencepost, and off to the side, the yawning of the open gate.

A cool breeze from the field, the distant braying of the animals.

While Martin knelt in his own vomit on the tarmac, besmirching his Sunday best, Celia walked as if in a dream toward the figure that lay broken behind the car, bathed in the red of the brake-lights.

She was smiling, the body. A small pale dark-haired woman, facing Celia, almost a mirror of herself—in fact, for a moment, Celia did feel as if she was looking in a broken mirror, one arm bent backwards across a naked torso, legs positioned demurely, as if the body was just relaxing there. Most of the mortified flesh was hidden out of sight, but in the red light the body's smile looked a little too wide, and it was true, the cheeks had been torn ragged.

And the eyes were staring, glistening in the red light.

"Oh God, Oh GOD" Martin howled.

Celia turned and saw the passenger door of the car shut closed. She screamed, and Martin turned as well, ostensibly to look at her, but in the process he caught a glimpse of the man reaching across to him from the passenger's seat. A haggard mask bedevilled by age and overgrown white hair, a shock on top of the head and growing from the lower half of the face.

A baby's glee in the expression, the body naked and pockmarked. All Celia saw was a pair of muscled arms reach out and pull her husband, struggling, into the car.

Valkyrie Loughcrewe

Now, watch for this
because something fascinating occurs here inside Celia's mind.
the situation unfolding splits, duplicates,
mitosis of the consciousness
It's nothing like a split-image effect in a film, not as if the
observer within her
is sitting in a darkened, smoke-filled theatre watching a pair of
screens
each showing a slightly different cut of the same film
no, she is experiencing both simultaneously
and fully
In one life she screams as the SUV rocks
Martin's screams becoming strangled.

in another, she screams for a different reason.
over the barbed wire, through the bushes,
from the gate, from the swung open doors
of the vehicle, come pale figures
like the one her husband struck
indistinctly formed, perfectly illuminated
by no light, flailing toward her
as in the other life, she calls out for
Martin one final, pathetic time,
hears the sound of the gear shift,
and the SUV reverses toward her at speed.

A single neural impulse fired—shared across the vast gulf between those twin experiences, those parallel lives—to turn, and to run. Both instances were too slow, far too slow, as Celia turned in a blur, in slow motion, the red light of the SUV creeping up on her, the horde of flailing, drowning-victim screams just a breath away.

The body stared up with the sightless eyes, smiling, as from the darkness above her another vision emerged, into the red light, a skinny body hanging from a bloated head, ballooning beyond the limits of her vision, pore-pocked with glistening black eyes, pulling the night around it like a cloak.

and the fourth collision

Slide 2:

Unveiling of the Acolyte

Still with me?
Good. Let us move our focus to this—a little compound up in the
hills that might look for all the world like a dairy farm. You've
got the acres of land, a pair of barns, and you can even smell
the manure and hear the milling about of the handful of cows
that the owner keeps alive through the labours of a rotating cast
of servants. Despite the facade, this place is anything but a
farm.
But you already knew that, didn't you?

The day was hot and bleary, the grass parched, even
yellowing in places, and there were patches of muck-turned
dust here and there across the junk-strewn front yard of the
compound, the kind that could give an ecologically minded type a
scare, sending their mind toward thoughts of drought and
desertification.

The trio of people who arrived that noon were anything but
ecologically minded, being officers of the Garda Siochana, there on
account of a neighbouring farmer's complaints of the mounting
pile of black bin-bags around the side of the owner's shed. At the
bottom of the hill, a sheep farmer and a farmer of dairy and fowl
had been beset by an ungodly reek carried on the breeze, and their
trips up to the site had met them only with confused day labourers
wringing their hands about being unable to organising the disposal
of the rubbish. The owner of the place was always just having left,
or away on business for a couple of days.

Garda intervention, in accordance with how things went in the
far-flung reaches of rural Ireland, did not come from a simple

neighbourly complaint—that was purview of the midlands. The pair of farmers had arrived at the house armed with a hammer and a rifle, blows were thrown, and a Sudanese fella by the name of Ali Siddiq ended up in hospital. As little as the small local garda presence enjoyed doing any work at all, they had to keep up some measure of appearances, and so that day they parked up on the driveway, and came face to face with Doctor Millard Whitehead.

It seems like part of you recognises him. Could that be because you can see, even without the insane shock of fuzzy hair and beard, that this clean-shaven man is the feral maniac who lurched toward Martin Campbell from the passenger seat of his own car?

"Hello gentlemen," he said, all flannel and sweat, wiping engine grease from his hands.
"I suppose you're here about the rubbish."

A convulsion in the patient.
You recognise the voice too, naturally.
Interesting you didn't have this kind of reaction
from the recording of his talk from the
2018 International Genetics Conference in Prague
"Evolutionary Psychology: The Genome of Meaning."
Perhaps you're only beginning to wake up now.

"Come on in for a cuppa, boys, let's talk it over," he said.
The cops glanced at each other, shrugged, and shuffled into the house.
"Jimmy Murphy down the road said one of your farm hands attacked him and Noel O'Donnell when they came up to try and talk to you about the smell coming off here," Garda Sergeant Phil McClaine said through a mouthful of chocolate biscuit.
"I don't want to argue, sir, but there are a pair of bullet-holes in my shed and a hospital bill that would indicate that our friends down the road are not exactly innocent here."
"Two sides to every story, isn't there?" McClaine responded.
"I see. Well, I must apologise. I'm barely home these days, I'm managing a lot of projects both here and overseas, and I failed to

realise that there was a discrepancy in my recycling account—which is now sorted out. I've been on to the county council, I have to pay a fine. And as far as my employee, these things happen. Water under the bridge. In fact I will personally apologise to Mr. Murphy and Mr. O'Donnell myself before I jet off again."

McClaine shook his head with a wry smile.

"And where are you jetting off to?" A younger lad by the name of Brian Walsh asked.

"Hong Kong," the man replied through a Mona Lisa smile."I have an investment in a laboratory that's been growing hamburgers out of stem cells. It's going quite well, but I like to go and learn as much as I can about the cutting edge of science and technology. Get my money's worth."

His smile did not falter a sliver as a great, sliding metallic crash came from outside.

"And there go the cows." He sighed.

A silence lingered for a moment, as if he expected the Gardai to excuse themselves.

"The young ones get rambunctious this time of year," he added.

"If you're always working abroad, why exactly are you keeping cows, mister . . . " The third officer, Peter Donaghy, asked.

"Whitehead," the doctor said, standing, moving to the kitchen window. "They're actually for research, studying the genes."

"What kind of r—" Brian started.

"That's enough," McClaine cut him off. "Sure look, sounds like you've got everything sorted here, we'll leave you to it."

"Nice of you to drop by, thank you—I will send proof of my correspondence with the council to your station."

"No need," the Sergeant said, waving him off.

A howl from outside; a guttural, multi-tone scream of desperation. The spines of all four men in the room shook with horror at the sound, it cut like a scalpel. The police raced into the garden, terror spurring them into action, and waiting for them there, stumbling, falling, crawling, standing again, across the parched grass, one asymmetrical hand grasping a handful of sand.

Naked, clumsy
Gasping, bloodied
One arm thick and hairy

Valkyrie Loughcrewe

Another shrinking at the elbow, becoming pale and smooth
Mismatched legs
A ring of scars at the neck, the elbows
The head having been removed and re-attached
To a reconfigured rib-cage
A patchwork, malcompleted puzzle

Doctor Millard Whitehead pulled a .22 pistol from his pocket and shot himself through the roof of his mouth. The police stared dumbfounded as the thing which escaped his second barn shrieked and writhed, burning in the sun.

The discovery of the thing that Whitehead had made of Martin Campbell prompted a full raid of the laboratory Whitehead had spent the previous decade assembling in his second barn. It was the most cutting-edge equipment available in the fields of genetics, cloning, and nanotechnology. Stem cell incubators and plastic wombs, a CRISPR system, a micro-laser for encoding gold molecules into bio-available nano-medicines, top of the line surgical equipment, a treasure trove of drugs, disinfectant, anti-virals, anti-bacterials, facilities for growing organs, bones and marrow.

Most perplexing of all, to the maddening horror of the Campbell family—of Martin's surviving wife Celia—was the fact that the experiments conducted upon him by Doctor Whitehead, international patron of science and technology, philosopher of the cutting edge of human endeavours, had left Martin heavily pregnant.

It would not be long until the birth, and what a birth it would turn out to be.

Patient has returned to a catatonic stupor
Holding off on introducing stimulants for now
But your gaze seems focused, that's good
I can work with that, for now

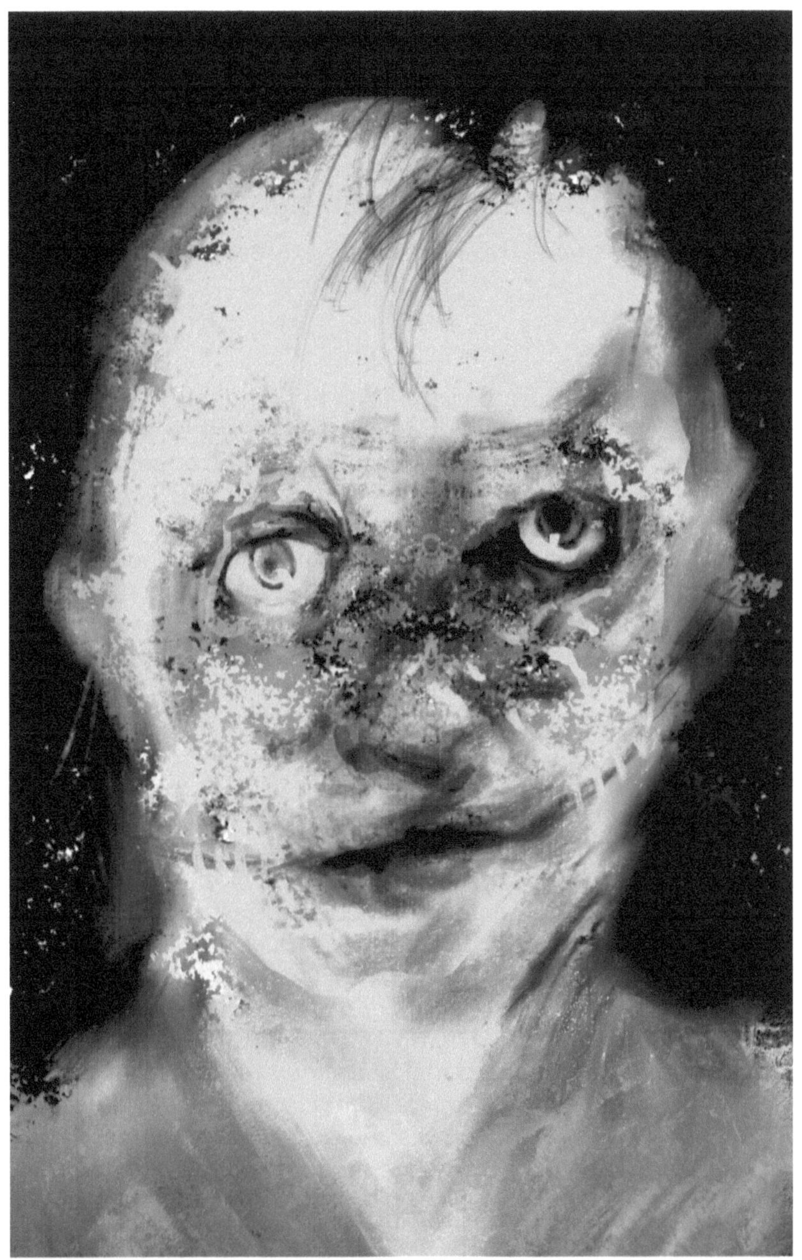

Slide 3:

Helical intubancy of the myopic stratum

Now we must turn our attention to the night in which poor Celia became faced with two equally terrible possibilities. Either her medication was beginning to fail, or her condition was worsening to the point of *if this is how I am now, what would I be like without these pills?*

She stood, shaking, standing in front of her empty, too-big bed, in her empty, too-big house, with so much empty lonely rural space around it, rain beating down on her windows. As far as we can see, she's simply standing facing her mirror, in her silken nightgown, mouth agape with tears streaming from her bugging eyes; but her reflection, though it may have been the trigger, was not what she saw.

At first she saw, as clear as day, replacing her reflection
A vision of the Virgin Mary clothed in baby blue
A stab of conflicting emotions, awe, hope,
Then horror, because the head of the Virgin
Was Martin's head, eyes rolled back and tongue lolling
The seizure he got so many years ago
From of all things, seasonal allergies
Repeated again, in her reflection, head copying
Her own movements as he claws at the Virgin's Robes
Peeling back layers of fabric, folds of bleeding flesh
Raw exposed inflamed internal membrane
Squirming with runnels of corruption
Drawing her deeper
Toward some inexorable horror

Puppet's Banquet

She had to drive herself to Doctor Kharmakar's office that day, as she did every day. What remained of her own family wanted nothing to do with her, disgusted as they were with what had happened. It was too indecent, too foul. Martin's family had found it in their hearts to assist with his medical expenses, to try and fix what had been done to him, but that did not extend to supporting Celia.

White-knuckled, her hands shook as she drove herself the two-and-a-half-hour journey to Dublin. Her mind felt like it was always teetering at the loopedge of a black void, or rather, that there was only one last sliver of grounding left, surrounded by a yawning chasm which had devoured everything else. What that grounding was, she was becoming less and less sure.

"Unfortunately, under international medical law we are unable to terminate this particular pregnancy." Kharmakar's voice cut through the fugue.

"Wh-what?" She asked, as confused by his statement as by her sense of missing time.

"The . . . Condition your husband has been put in is of an extreme rarity. I'm not speaking of a male pregnancy, it's the state of the embryo. It's developing in a way that has only been recorded once before in the history of humanity."

"I . . . I don't care!?" Celia exclaimed, anger battling with a sinking nausea. "A-and I'm sure Martin wouldn't either if you didn't have him in that bloody coma."

The tears came then, and Kharmakhar just kept talking, desperate to get it over with.

"It's what's known as an Ichneumon pregnancy—"

"Please, just put an end to it!"

"—also known as a Mandlebrot Conjoinment."

He slid a yellowed, crumbling pamphlet across the desk toward her. On it there was a medical diagram of the head of what could have been a human baby, if it had been put through a kaleidoscope, eyes and ears and vestigial mouths struggling for dominance on a mound of flesh which resembled a pinecone more than it did a skull.

Valkyrie Loughcrewe

"He can't have a child! Let alone this . . . thing."

"Children born this way can theoretically live full lives, and you and your husband—"

"Stop . . . Please . . . !"

The Ichneumon Birth and its Implications by Harrison Merryweather, 1903

"—will be able to avail of significant government supports. It's a lot of money, Mrs. Campbell"

Celia choked out a laugh, before covering her mouth. Of course it was. She had wished and wished that Martin would bring in more money, would work less, and all had come true—at the cost of his body, her sanity, and the laws of nature. Kharmakar gave her an odd look for a moment, before returning to his professional mask of neutrality.

"Martin's family is, upon medical advisory, transferring him to a specialist clinic–the Bannican institute on Inishee island. There will be arrangements made if you wish to stay by his side during the final few weeks of the process."

"I—no. I can't. I can't bear to see. I don't want to see it," she said, looking down at her hands.

"I think Martin would rather you were there when he woke up," the Doctor said softly.

"You don't know him," Celia spat. "None of you do. If you did, you'd walk up to him in that state and shoot him in the head."

Kharmakhar sighed.

"Well, there's a room for you there, at the institute, if you should change your mind. Mrs. Campbell, I obviously can't make any promises, but if anyone can fix Martin, it's the surgeons at Bannican."

"I'm—I'm sorry," Celia said.

She stood.

"No, Mrs. Campbell, you have nothing to apologise for," Doctor Kharmakhar said to a closing door.

On the walk back through the medical centre, Celia found herself wanting to grab someone, anyone, out of the small crowd of workers or patients-to-be, going about normal lives, with normal problems. She wanted to tell them that her husband had just been plucked out of her life by some kind of mad scientist and twisted into an abomination beyond anything they could imagine. She wanted to beg someone to rescue her from the nightmare her life had become, to give her a whole new set of circumstances, a whole new name, a whole new context to exist in.

Room to forget, to transform.

On the way out to the car she found herself stopping to stare at a flag which flew above a graffiti-strewn concrete wall. Something about its bright colours, their pattern and the way the material flapped desperately above the roll of razor-wire and glass shards which sat atop the wall made her stomach lurch, and her mind refused to let her move on until she understood why. She did not recognise the flag enough to name the country, did not remember where she had seen it before, but it had signalled something to her. Something perhaps about a wider world with wider crises than the twisted abnormality her tiny little life had become.

This thought only served to make her feel even more like somewhere along the line she had slipped off the edge of the world and found herself hanging from it by her fingertips. A stranger jostling to get past her saved her from this stupor, and she moved on.

The drive home was all shafts of orange light cutting through titans of dark clouds turned pale by the dusk. The abyss within her told her that there was something up there watching her, something foul and hell-bent on perverting everything the light touched. Every car driving through the bleary patches of light would be cursed, rearranged and reconfigured by the diseased child that had taken God's throne. She allowed herself to pass through the beams with tremulous hands on the wheel, foot pulled away from the brake.

She would not allow herself to break, not on the fucking M50. It wouldn't have mattered anyway, she had already been cursed.

She imagined the warped husk of her husband—

Parts of his rib cage, his arms, one leg, several organs, spinal tissue replaced with parts from either another body or even potentially grown within the machinery of the lab he escaped from—medicated, unconscious, drowning in nightmares, as they transported him by helicopter across the sea—

Valkyrie Loughcrewe

*A parasitic horror growing inside the incubator they shoved
into his body, a blackened anti-miracle, a curse, a suppurating
pool of pseudo-human malformation congealing within him*
She wished that she had died that night, that Martin was dead;
and as she arrived home she vomited bile onto the pavement as
the last of the light slipped away.
It would live, it would be happy and healthy. It would be loved.

The only thing left to be done was to care for the child, as she'd
done since he was born. She met the babysitter at the door, who
smiled sadly at her through an overstuffed mouth of yellow teeth.
The crying began the moment she stepped into the front hall.

It's too cold in here, the babysitter should have had the heat on!

She turned around to complain, but the door was already open
on an empty driveway. She hurried to turn all the radiators on,
warm up some milk in a plastic cup, the baby's crying ringing in
her ears. Her breathing was shallow, thoughts fragmented and
anxious. She needed to fulfil her baby's need to be with mother, to
be fed, to be held.

She entered the cracked-robins-egg blue baby room, with its
hanging mobiles, soft carpeted floor, wall of teddy bears and in the
centre, a large comfortable bed with the small form of her child.
She rushed to him, feeling his cold, spindly arms wrap around her,
hearing him coo as the wailing subsided. As mother arrived.

That was the moment she remembered that she and Martin
never had a baby.

Little fingers scrabble like insects and the grip turns tight
The O of her mouth screams soundlessly
Can't hurt the baby Can't hurt
She rips away, and the arms rip away with her
Milk spills all over the sheets, sourly reeking
And she turns and runs for the door,
So far away across a sea of shattered
Powder blue eggshells
Only a glimpse she got
Who was the babysitter she met at the door?

Puppet's Banquet

Who had been inside her house
With a burnt hamburger face shoved full of
Cornhusk teeth?
Only a glimpse of the armless totem pole thing
In the blue bed looking at her, hurt and teary
Crying sweetly as the stumps of its missing arms
Haemmorhage something not quite fluid

Celia spent that night in bed trying to shut out the cries of the degrading hallucination, and somewhere along the line she decided that an institute was where she needed to be. Somewhere with doctors and white walls, away from everything. She decided that she was going to go there, to Bannican, to see Martin, to get help.

After all, Martin was all she had. Her mother was long dead, her father barely sentient, his brains riddled with disease, his vast empire a crab bucket of middle managers and boards of directors, his houses lying empty and tied up in foreign money, the machinery of his factories winding down. There were no siblings, the cousins gone off to foreign shores to seek their fortune, closing the gates of communication behind them as they went. And she herself, incapable, tiny, no savings, no investments, no future. She would fade away, slip between the cracks.

All the while, she would be feeling those fingers scrabbling across her shoulder blades, those cold arms gripping her, like the pulled off legs of a weevil, still stuck to the material of her body.

As morning light returned, and she crept out of her room with a bag full of clothes for the trip, she noticed that the door to the baby room was still there. She did not look back as she pulled out of the driveway.

It is beginning to occur to us that in your haggard state,
your interpretation of what you're being shown may not fit the
reality
of what actually transpired.
Be advised that
there is no room for subjectivity in this process.
You must witness fully
You must understand

Slide 4:

Flatigious Somnambulistic Promulgation

From fighting for his life
To awakening suffocated
Transited via acrid chemical fumes
His throat chafing on tubing
His eye misplacing slightly as it swivels
Phantom limbs, phantom heart,
Phantom lungs
All he feels is plastic tubing
Violate his severed skull,
Pumping fluids into his veins
His brain
All he sees is misted glass
Until a white-gloved hand wipes it clear
And a grinning face stares in

Martin woke up yelling in his hospital bed, a barbaric glossolalia of yelps bursting from his parched throat. He stared up at closed curtains, seafoam green, and to the wood-panelled ceiling above. His mind rapid-fire shuffled through a carnival of horrors, all sterile white and blood red, and that leering, softly spoken figure who would let him wake for brief periods, to look at himself sliced open—watching new bones, new organs transplanted.

Watching his belly grow.

"You're awake." A woman's voice came from outside the curtain.

He stared for a moment at the ceiling, eyes bulging. What should he say? Had he really managed to escape, or had that been a dream? Was the person across from him another captive of the psychopath, doomed to the same kinds of torture and violation he had endured in fits and starts of consciousness across a time period he couldn't ascertain?

"Or are you? Hello?" The voice came again.

"Where am I?" He said, his voice cracked, pitch off, but not quite as warped as he expected.

"You're safe. You're in a really fancy hospital. Nobody would tell me what happened to you, but I guess it was something pretty bad, right?"

He couldn't place the accent. Waterford? Galway?

"Celia . . . " He groaned, the words coming before the thought even arose. "Is she . . ."

"I don't know anything about that, I'm sorry. We can ask the nurse when she comes in, she should have done her checkup by now, maybe she's running late."

"Did they fix me?"

"I don't know. You sound like you need a drink of water."

His body felt so heavy, he couldn't even move his fingers, move his head, let alone sit up.

"I'm Jill, by the way. What's your name?"

"Martin."

The kick came then, a small, but firm and definite thump in his belly—in his womb.

"Jesus fucking christ!" He groaned, his voice rising to a scream. "Jesus CHRIST get this fucking THING OUT OF ME!"

The kicking increased, the parasite inside him gleeful at his misery, and Martin found in his adrenaline surge the strength to move, to grip the sides of his bed and pull his legs across to the side, and he saw it then, huge, heavy, hijacking his body to incubate itself.

His feet hit a cold floor, and he thought he could hear Jills voice calling his name, *Martin, Martin!* He pushed through the curtain, getting tangled in it, ripping it away, casting it aside.

It was a high-ceilinged but small ward, enough for only three beds. The floor linoleum was standard but the walls and ceiling were wood panelled, and on the wall there was a huge realist painting of an island battered by a stormy sea.

He was alone in the room. The bed from which the voice had come was empty, uncurtained.

His spine immediately groaned, his whole body sending him

alarms, and he moved toward the double doors out of the ward, calling for someone, anyone to help, his words rapidly degenerating into the grunts and hooting of a crippled animal.

The hallway was long, and dimly lit, and quiet save for the murmuring of machines; it was every hospital corridor he had ever been in at night. When he sat vigil over his mother as she wasted away, when he listened as in the other room his sister screamed his nephew into the world.

He gripped the walls as he walked, barely able to support his own weight, and there was an impression of people, a sense of movement around him, but he saw no faces, felt no hands reaching out to stop him.

"Martin . . ." Disbelief in her voice, a sob followed—it was Celia.

He looked up, and she was there, standing in the middle of the waiting room, at the end of the hall, surrounded by grey people in grey clothes living grey lives. Her eyes were wide, streaming tears, and she opened her arms to him as he lurched toward her.

"Celia!" He screamed, his voice harsh, undignified, the voice of a startled toddler.

"Mar—"

Her mouth twitched, and she shuddered, her fingers locking unnaturally, and something changed. The clammy air got colder, and something strange happened to the face of someone sitting away in the corner, like it moved an inch lower than the rest of their head.

Celia was turning grey, and the baby stopped kicking, and the tiny hairpin cracks started spreading from the points in her head where the pale stalks began to grow. They grew like mollusc antennae, out from her head, from her arms, and Celia and the other grey people crumbled to ash as the fungal growths that hid within them spread in a living time-lapse to greet their halogen sun.

Martin woke up yelling in his hospital bed, a barbaric glossolalia of yelps bursting from his parched throat. He stared up at closed curtains, seafoam green, and to the wood-panelled ceiling above. He was slick with sweat, and in his mouth, he tasted ashes.

"You tried to leave, didn't you?" Jill asked from beyond the curtain.

Patient is drifting into delusion,
Administering amphetamines.

Slide 4(b):

Insidious Remnant Configuration

Now, become aware of the marred, off-white shape of the five o'clock ferry from Dowth village to Inishee island. If it weren't for the thick sheets of rain and dark veils of fog, we could probably make out more of the isle and its surrounding treacherous reefs, rising up out of the sea in a wedge, its gentle incline giving way to immense cliffs. On a clear day we could probably even see the very tip of the highest peaked, neo-classical styled rooftop of the Bannican institute.

There were few people on the ferry with Celia—quiet, older people on their way to the island with bags of goods from the mainland to haul back to their sleepy island lives. Celia watched the rain beat down against the double-layered window, fascinated by the dearth of dead spiders and their stale webs that had collected between the panes over who-knew-how-many years. She wondered if it had ever been cleaned.

She allowed the crewmen to drive her car down onto the pier, and as it trundled down the rickety metal ramp, she looked across the sea, into the wall of fog, the churning black waters and she could almost feel the tumult of the waves, the foam of their clashing in her blood. A sadistic self-destructive urge came upon her, then, and she stared into the abyss within her, daring it to conjure up some horror from the churning brine, something to plummet her into madness and free her from her responsibilities.

No such horror came. The nice old man from the Ferry handed over her keys through the window, got out, and then she was away. The small island town gave way quickly to extremely tight, winding lanes obscured by overhanging trees and tall branches, forcing

Valkyrie Loughcrewe

Celia to crawl along at a snail's pace for fear that some local would come careening around the bend in a tractor, unused to the sudden presence of a visitor driving up their road.

The road never widened, but the world around her soon did, the oppressive vegetation and driveways into secluded island homes giving way to a rolling craggy expanse of moss, of mist, of silver lakes, crumbling ruins of old houses, wandering sheep. A pair of ghostly headlights precluded a rattling, rusting pickup which came chugging into Celia's way, forcing her to take refuge in a gravelly strip off to the side of the road which threatened, if she was to position herself poorly, to send her car rolling down a steep bank towards God knew what.

The higher she got, the more the sun broke through the clouds, the thinner the fog became, and the clearer the Bannican Institute loomed. She had expected some kind of sleek modern campus, all glass and steel, but what she saw getting closer was an old brownstone relic of the colonial past—closer to Oxford than any building she had ever seen in Ireland.

It was an absurdity, perched there at the flattened top of the wedge-shaped isle, amidst the wave-battered cliffs which came into full view as the fog lifted, and the tilting, warped landscape careening toward the myriad colossal drop-offs into the glittering Atlantic.

The scale of it all, for a moment, snatched her mind out from the quagmire of diseased horror that her life had become, and placed her looking down on herself, a small and fragile animal piloting a slight contraption to the only hospitable path through a vast and hostile geography, rising from endless black depths.

The road finally levelled out and widened, the crumbling tarmac getting smoother, turning to fine gravel as Celia arrived in the gardens of the Bannican institute. There were flowers in the front, and rose gardens around the side, and grand but simple water features, artistic configurations of bowls pouring water, and ponds full of lilies.

She parked her car. The lot was surprisingly full, and she wondered how those who worked in the institute commuted, if they lived on the island. Her eyes were drawn to a bizarre sight in the rose garden as a pair of figures emerged from behind a viny trellis.

One was dressed in a pristine white clean-suit—their face obscured by a glass visor, their hands covered in thick white gloves. There was an oxygen tank at their side, attached to the mask, and they were holding the hand of an old, decrepit figure, a man in a white gown with long, wispy white hair and a long white beard, whose lips shuddered as he put one bare foot in front of the other, looking down at the ground.

She wondered why someone would need a hazmat suit to walk an old man. Was he contagious with some kind of disease? Would she be at risk stepping out of the car in his presence?

She closed her eyes and shook her head. Another hallucination, surely, but upon re-opening the vision persisted. The two figures slipped away into a grove of apple trees.

She emerged from the car, breathing the sea air and feeling the gravel crunch under her shoes, and she went around to grab her wheelie bag from the boot. Her mind, still somewhat impressed upon by the scale of the landscape she had just traversed, was beginning to set into a neutrality, an acceptance.

This had become her life, this had befallen her husband, but perhaps it *could* be remedied. Perhaps strange and foul things occurred in the shadowy corners of the world every day, unreported, and perhaps that was because there were places like the Bannican institute, secreted on high, at the fringes, ready to make the problems go away, unreported, best forgotten.

Just like you, and just like me.

Creeping uncertainty assailed her newfound sense of peace with every step toward the front steps of the building. A pair of thick purple double doors lay open to the vast reception hall of the institute. The centrepiece of the room was a bronze statue of a caduceus, with its twin winding serpents. The statue loomed above a round pewter receptionist's desk, and itself was made to seem smaller by the height of the landing above it and the great round windows which let the glow of natural light pierce the stony gloom.

A pale young woman in a dark blue suit greeted her with a smile.

"Hello! Are you visiting?" She asked cheerily.

"Um . . . " Celia paused, thrown off by the idea of meeting a new person and immediately associating herself with the unspeakable.

"Can I get your name?" The receptionist asked, her smile unwavering.

Celia's chest felt tight, and at the edges of her vision it seemed there were people standing up on the landing, leering down at her, lining the twin half-moon staircases, watching, judging. The receptionist's smile was too steady, like she was a doll, a mannequin created to represent something as opposed to a living human, writhing with internal contradiction and hideous urges.

Celia took a breath.

"Celia Campbell," she said.

The receptionist thanked her, and took a moment tapping away at her computer. She frowned, and the tightness returned in Celia's chest again.

"I—is something wrong?" Celia asked.

The smile returned as the receptionist remembered she was in the presence of another, and she looked up at Celia with eyes that said something else.

"Not at all. Let me just check something."

Her hands went below the lip of the desk, to an old yellowed notepad that Celia could not see, several pages down. She nodded, with an affirmative, performative *mhm*, and looked back up to Celia.

"Ah yes, Mrs. Campbell, we can show you to your room straight away, and on the way we'll let you know about visiting hours, dinner and breakfast, and everything else. Is that okay?"

In short order, a thin man in a white uniform who looked at once middle aged and barely out of his teens greeted her, and took her walking through the institute. His shiny brass name-tag read "Sam".

"Your husband is staying in Ward C of the west wing, but I'm afraid he is undergoing treatment today, and will not be available for visitation until tomorrow evening."

"What kind of treatment?" She wondered, holding her tongue against what she ached to say next.

What kind of treatment could he possibly need aside from
an abortion—or euthanasia?

"I believe the doctors are preparing his body for restoration from how it was altered, which will begin once the main procedure has taken place."

The birth.

"So there is a way to fix him?" Celia asked.

"I can't make any promises, I'm just an orderly. But the doctors here are very good at what they do."

The corridors of the hospital barely resembled a hospital; they all had the look of a lavish stately home. Every hall and chamber they passed through was bathed in powder blue daylight which streamed in through tall, panelled windows. Despite the size of the place, Celia saw very few people as she followed the orderly, save for a nurse wheeling a tray of pills and paper cups through a pair of large mahogany doors.

She tried to get a glimpse of the room inside, but the doors shut silently in her face as she passed.

"Down the stairs to the left there is the cafeteria," Sam told her. "We serve dinner at 7pm and breakfast at 9am, and now we are passing just above the conservatory which houses the Bannican art gallery. A new work will be unveiled tomorrow, a very fine piece by an anonymous donor."

Before she knew it, Celia was standing with that strange, white suited orderly in front of a single white door, at the end of a gloomy third floor corridor lit only by a small round porthole window at the end.

"And this will be your room, Ms. Odessa."

Odessa? The word made her head throb.

"Uh, Campbell," Celia corrected him. "My name is Celia Campbell."

Her words came out slurred. The orderly tilted his head, a curious look on his face, and then he smiled. Celia blinked, and a black dot danced in her vision.

"Of course, you should get some rest. I'll see you at dinner, I'm sure."

Celia tried to say something, tried to turn and use the door, but she felt rooted to the spot, her executive function flailing in the form of phantom limbs, a phantom voice, a waking sleep paralysis. She felt her eyes moving, and though her vision was still, the black dot followed, and her head hurt, and the pain came from the dot.

"Get some rest rest." The orderly said again, repeating. "Rest rest get some Odessa of course i'll see i'm sure rest get some—"

Not again.

Celia's heart spiked as she ripped herself away from the moment, her perception once again bisecting, one Celia falling through the door into her room, stumbling for a great big bed more luxurious than from any hotel she had ever stayed in, the other Celia stuck juddering in the hallways as the orderly's head tilted ceaselessly, nauseatingly, repeating—

Get some rest get some rest get some rest
Odessa

One Celia burrowed into the covers, pressed a pillow to her face, around her ears, breathed deeply and loudly, but she couldn't drown out the other self. She still saw, she still heard, still felt with every cell of her body the stale air of the gloomy corridor, and in the darkness that enveloped one set of her eyes the blot danced even darker, radiating pain.

Even as she began to drift into sleep, the face of the orderly remained, dissolving slowly into ergotic patterns, shimmering tendrils of iridescent colour which swallowed her up, becoming a dream too alien to recall.

Dr. Bethany McGuire, MD:
Testimony I

I didn't think I'd have it in me to do something like this. I've seen so much, let so much go in my time in the profession that I really thought that for it to come to this, well . . . I'm not afraid of being implicated any more. The victims need justice.

I'm willing to give names, reports, point authorities in any direction I can, but I'm . . . I don't know what authorities can even help at this point. I will get to all that, believe me. I—I just need to sit down and open up that vault in my head where I've let all this condense and compress, all this repressed shit, all this evil that I've witnessed, and write it all down. The abuse of patients, the cruelty. The psychopathy of almost everyone working in that city, their methods, their victims—and if I'm to go down with them, so be it. I deserve it.

Before that, however, I need to talk about what has pushed me to this point. The unethical—

(subject laughs)

—God, unethical doesn't even begin to cover it. The abhorrent . . . things . . . What can I even call them?

It. The structure. The abhorrent underlying

Valkyrie Loughcrewe

structure of what this hospital even *does* goes beyond anything I could have even imagined, even after what I saw in the US. They think they're so beyond the curve here that they've lost any regard for human morality.

These aren't patients. They're cattle. It may look like they're being treated well, some are even being given the appearance of being cured and released, but they're not really leaving. Nobody really leaves this place. I . . .

(there is a long moment of silence from Dr. McGuire. In the background, muffled talking and bustling can be heard, indicating that she may be recording from inside an empty room in the hospital during work hours)

I don't know why I'm even doing this. They're in everything now. This goes beyond paying off cops and a conspiracy of silence. They're behind the walls. They take their orders from—

Oh, I didn't realise somebody was in here.

No, it's alright, I was just on a call. I'm finished now.

Slide 5:

Narcolepsis Amalgamation

You're slipping again.
I want to know this time, I want you to speak to me your
delusions.
There's a lot we can learn from each other.

A small, olive-pale face peering out from behind a curtain. Eyes wide, expression uncertain.

A red, tear-streaked face across the way, peering out in kind.

"You . . . Weren't there when I got up," the red-faced man spoke.

"I didn't hear you get up, I heard them come for you," Jill responded.

"Them?" Martin asked.

"I don't want to think about that, I—" Jill trailed off.

"*Who* came for me?" Martin asked, his voice cracking.

"I don't know. I was afraid to look. You were screaming, and they didn't speak."

"That didn't happen, that *didn't happen, Jill.*"

He reached through the curtain, gripping the bedframe with his other hand for support.

"Can—can you take my hand? Maybe we can get out, together?"

"I don't *want* to leave. They're taking care of me, and they're probably going to take care of you too. I won't last long with how fast my condition is worsening."

"Jill, I walked out there, and there were people with things growing out of their heads, crumbling into dust."

Valkyrie Loughcrewe

The olive-pale face retracted back into the curtain.

"It was just a nightmare, Martin. I've had them too. We're going to be okay, they're going to make us better."

"Jill, I was cut apart and sewn back together with other body parts. My head was taken off my body, and he put a *womb* in me. I'm *pregnant.*"

There was a long pause.

"I don't think I'm going to be getting better," he said, to no response.

The silence spoke to him, and it said that his roommate didn't believe him. He lay back, feeling his organs squirm under the pressure of his swollen womb. His breath became shallow, and his whole body tensed in anticipation of feeling the thing kick.

He stared up at the cream coloured ceiling tiles, his mouth stuck open, voice rasping and—

Wasn't the ceiling made of wood before? A tile popped out of place, sliding aside slowly, painfully slowly, and something pattered against his face, it tasted sour and salty at the same time, and something wet and pink and veiny distended from the darkness above, raining foul fluid onto Martin's face.

He jerked to the side, trying to scramble out of bed, and felt his vertebrae heave from the extra weight. He fell over the side this time, the pain knocking the wind out of him, the impact from his pregnant belly sending shockwaves throughout his body.

Fingers scrabbling against something thick and greasy coating a cold metal floor, legs quivering in agony. His mouth flapped, and his mind could only produce a single thought.

I hope you die.

He heard the squeal of sliding doors open. He rasped for Jill as heavy footsteps reverberated across the floor, the metal vibrating as if it were a thin platform suspended above a void.

Rough hands grabbed Martin, and he was being lifted to his feet, the bright lights of the room searing his vision. Still, he saw the bed in front of him. A stained, rusted surgical table, the straps open, waiting for him. The lower half of the table split off wide, the ankle straps as far apart as they could get, and between them, a basin of black liquid.

Not a surgical table. A birthing table.

The foetus kicked, weak and broken, a wave of nausea ripping through his body.

The rough hands became a softness which held him, taking the weight of his body, and his vision blurred, and he knew he was returning to his ward, to the quiet room, with Jill.

He woke, and turned, and vomited off the side of the bed. He watched the clear liquid spatter into an immaculately placed silver bedpan.

"You're not making it up, are you?" Jill asked.

Martin looked up, mouth dribbling bile, to see her looking out again from behind the curtain.

"Are we dead?" He asked.

"I sure hope not." Jill sighed. "I have shit to do."

"Tell me about it," said Martin, wiping his mouth.

He scanned the room as he could see from his bed. The act exhausted him. Wooden walls and ceiling, one door. Heavy curtains blocking the window, wall-lamps lighting the room, and more heavy-duty fluorescents above, switched off. One single door leading out.

"How long has it been since we first started talking?" Martin asked.

"I don't know. A few hours? A night?"

"What happened to me just there?"

"You vomited."

"I fell out of bed, I saw things, I felt—people. You're not telling me that I'm just having nightmares, you have experienced things like that, haven't you? Getting out of bed and then things getting weird?"

"I don't know."

"You said it to me when it first happened. You asked me if I tried to leave!"

"Martin. I never said that." Jill said, her voice soft, sympathetic.

Martin paused for a moment, and sighed deeply. He felt tears coming, he felt big heaving sobs swimming to the surface.

"Just wait for the nurse to come, she'll see that you're awake and get the doctors. Everything's going to be okay."

Valkyrie Loughcrewe

He sobbed like a child, feeling the emotions thunder through his body, and in his mind's eye he saw that that table, with the strap-buckles rusted stiff, and the waiting basin of still, dark water.

> *Nobody is coming to help me*
> *They have no intention of stopping this*
> *I'm going to suffer until something is done.*

He forced himself to make his crying as quiet as he could, so as not to upset Jill, and as his grip tightened on his emotions, his body slowly came to heel. Something was wrong, everything was wrong.

> *There's no way I'm not dead.*
> *That this isn't some kind of purgatory or even hell.*
> *The voice in my head, the spirit in my gut tells me*
> *That to lie still is to rot.*

Martin parted the curtain again, slightly. Jill was sequestered behind her partition, no longer peering out, and beyond the single door out into the hall, he could hear bustling, distant sounds of clinking metal, movement of things. Like a real hospital.

> *Same voice that told me that whatever happened,*
> *However grim things looked,*
> *That there was a plan, and that everything would be ok.*

He heaved his massive bulk around as quietly as he could—springs squeaking, material shifting. He didn't want to alarm Jill, and part of him had become suspicious that she was somehow his captor as much as his fellow captive.

> *Intuition, guardian angel, Jesus, Mary, God, the Holy Spirit*
> *tells me that this isn't how it seems.*
> *Your salvation is just around the corner.*
> *Yours, and Celia's.*

His swollen feet once again touched the cold ground, and as he shifted his bulk toward standing, his joints cracking as they settled, he realised that he was ravenously hungry. He walked toward the door, the sound of footsteps coming down the hall toward him.

> *If I'm dead, let me be free of this nightmare and find peace*
> *If God is out there, lead me to find his outstretched hand and*
> *take it.*
> *If I'm in hell, bring out the devil to break the news to me himself.*
> *And if I'm just going crazy, can somebody*
> *for the love of Christ*
> *Just fucking explain what's happening to me?*

His fingers reached the handle. It was cold. He pushed the door open.

> *This intersects with something.*
> *I need to draw you back toward the screen.*

Slide 6a:

Stendhaloidal Haemmorhagic Beatitude:
Princeps

Celia woke and marvelled at the room. The bed was a four-poster, the only of the kind she had ever seen in her life, let alone slept in. The ceiling was high and curved, and the furniture looked antique, complete with dressing table and changing screen.

Furthermore, there was an en-suite bathroom, and through the open door there wafted a balmy breeze which carried the scent of the sea.

Celia rose, feeling the sheet slide across her body, and she realised that she was naked, though she didn't remember taking off her clothes. She recoiled from the realisation that there was a full-length mirror in the corner of the room. She hated having to see her own body at the best of times, and in the split second she saw herself, she saw scars and mutilations running all down across her torso, unsightly bulges pulsating, flesh creeping.

She padded across the cold wooden floor of the room and threw a sheet across it without looking. Her heart's thudding calmed, and she shivered. She opened the wardrobe and found that it was full of ugly looking clothing. Jackets, scarves, gloves looking to be from the '60s or '70s. She reached in and her hand found a silk night-gown. She shut her eyes and tried it on. It fit perfectly.

Celia walked to the window of her room and opened it. Her room was up so high, higher than she'd expected. She wondered if it was in one of the turret-like spires she saw emerging from the top of the building. It was still early, the sun rising, casting the sky into a globular orange glow. The light seared into her eyes, creating neon-green trails which blossomed outward into delirious fractal images. Her head spun, her stomach rumbled, and the skyline above the glittering sea was suddenly a renaissance painting of angels playing an assortment of string instruments and horns.

She blinked, once, twice, but the hallucination remained. The skyline was a masterpiece, a Da Vinci, she could almost hear the music on the breeze, coming in waves of bleary sound. She wished that she could paint or sketch what she was seeing, but she knew to try would be to profane the image, for there amidst the crowd of heralding angels, she saw the tiny form of her mother, the same as she looked in the old photos of her years of Sean-nós, dancing to the pipes and lutes of heaven.

Celia sighed, a smile creeping across her face. The madness she had been afflicted with was not all bad, it seemed. And with that, a shadow passed across the sun, and the vision was replaced by a misty grey sky over the Atlantic. Celia shivered, feeling a tear rolling down her face.

What to do with such an experience?
Preach about it from the rooftops, to the patients? To the sea?
Burrow into logic to escape the delirium of mystic zeal?
Or take the Irish route, that people of a thousand brushed-off
bumps in the night, a million scoffed at visions, innumerable
dreamtime prophecies
That being, to just get on with it.
To just say,

"Feck it," Celia grunted.

She showered that morning in the ensuite, squinting, barely touching herself, letting the water pressure and the heat do all the work in the moment, finishing the job with a thick coating of antiperspirant and perfume, as she'd always showered. It surprised her how well stocked the bathroom was, with soaps and shampoos, perfume and everything else. She knew that the hospital was expensive, operated on the highest levels of medical science, but she didn't expect an Irish institution of any kind to skip on austerity where it could reasonably get away with it.

When she stepped out of the door into that cramped carpeted hallway which connected her to the rest of the building, she was, of course, dressed in her own clothes. She would not risk getting in trouble for wearing what had been left behind in the wardrobe or the dresser, though she couldn't really think of a reason why she would. She floated on a cloud of perfume into the main body of the institute, breathing through any thoughts of Martin or her blossoming madness that threatened to arise. Years of yoga down at the wellness centre had done more for her than reduce her backache, it seemed.

> *Light streams through the windows*
> *Treading through the beams*
> *Clad in old beige for an old maid*
> *Destined for bedlam*
> *at best*

She took the first stairs she found, letting her hand slide across the fine polished wood and taking in the landscape paintings that lined the walls on the way down, all depictions of the island, its town and its beaches. A faint smell of breakfast hit her nostrils as she descended to the ground floor, the sun dazzling her, glinting off a hundred golden flourishes in the wall-siding, the picture frames, the trimming of the carpet.

There were others there, milling about in the conservatory across from her, a couple of patients, one very thin and one quite obese, accompanied by relatives and orderlies. A woman in a pale grey uniform walked by Celia with a tray of food, heading up the stairs. Her nose wrinkled as she was assailed by the force of Celia's acrid chemical aura.

The conservatory was host to that art gallery the man had mentioned to Celia the night before. The work was striking, even from a distance. A semi-translucent partition wall held several portraits, the one which drew her eye the most being of a black man in dustbowl garb playing a weathered old guitar in front of a stove fire, the orange glow contrasting with the blue moonlight playing over the man and his instrument.

Celia's stomach grumbled. Art appreciation could wait. She had to eat. She was already going insane, it wouldn't be any more pleasant on an empty stomach. Hell, maybe the problem was that she hadn't been eating enough in the first place. Brains played tricks on people when they didn't eat, right? Not wishful thinking at all, Celia. Not wishful thinking at all.

She followed her nose down the hall, seeing a patient being wheeled from one door to another; a patient that she could have sworn was an old man, wrinkly to the point of being all ridges and pits, with *two heads*. One lolled back in the chair catatonic and the other alert and staring. Another hallucination, perhaps? Celia had seen a documentary once on a pair of conjoined twins in America that looked for all the world like a girl with two heads, and this was a place where they take patients with extremely unusual conditions, so it wasn't out of the question.

Regardless, wherever they were wheeling him, it wasn't where she was going.

The canteen was as lush as the rest of the building, a wide hall with polished wooden floors, high ceilings, and big patio doors letting in natural light, complemented by softly glowing hanging lamps. The smell hit her like a truck. A malty, savoury, bakery smell intermingled with trails of confectionery and rumbles of fine cooked meat and melted cheese, and there were not one, but two stations where food was being served. Most within looked to be wearing the white, blue, or pink garb of hospital attendants, with a couple of people in civilian attire, most likely relatives of patients. She wondered where the patients had their meals. Considering the condition some of these people were in, surely it was better to separate them from those who would have to look at them while eating.

She got into line, and when her turn came she heaped up her tray with a plate of pesto slathered almond bread slices, streaks of sizzling bacon, and a scrambled egg and avocado wrap, with some baked beans on the side. There was no till, nobody waiting by to see if she took too much. It was all free. She moved to the coffee machine, and looked out the patio windows into the hospital courtyard. There was a sprawling garden in which they seemed to be growing vegetables and flowers, sustenance and aesthetics being given equal attention. There she did see a handful of patients milling about, watched over by attendants. From where she stood, the only abnormality she could make out among them was one woman who seemed oddly tall, but that was about it.

Perhaps they've been cured already, Celia thought. *Or perhaps their illnesses aren't as visible as having two heads or a body that's been sewn back together wrong.*

"Mrs. Campbell?" A soft voice spoke from behind her.

It was Sam, the man who'd called her the wrong name last night. Her stomach lurched at the memory. She needed to sit down and get some breakfast into her. Sam smiled at her, though his brow was furrowed with concern.

"I don't mean to distract you from your breakfast, but please, if you'd come sit with me there's someone I'd like to introduce you to."

She followed to a large round table with only one person sitting at it, a woman who seemed to be around Celia's age, but whose face was clearly worn by stress. She looked up at the pair and smiled a weary smile as they approached.

"Celia, this is Doctor Janet Perrez, she is the surgeon in charge of your husband's recovery. She is the world's foremost expert in . . . his condition."

"It's nice to meet you, Celia," Janet said.

The way Sam stumbled over his words set Celia on edge. Was this Doctor an expert in reconfiguring a body that had been hacked apart and set back together? Or was she more invested in birthing the abominable thing which grew within him? Celia couldn't help but assume the latter, but she held on to her manners and sat.

"Will you be able to fix him?" Celia asked bluntly. "Will we be able to go back to normal?"

Doctor Perrez set down her fork and took a breath.

"I won't lie to you, Mrs.Campbell. With any kind of surgery there is a risk. If all things go well, yes. We can return your husband to the state he was in before this was inflicted on him. But it will be complicated, and it will be dangerous."

"Will he be more or less likely to survive if you were to abort the . . . thing inside him?"

"Celia—" Sam spluttered. "You must have been told that that isn't—"

"I know!" She snapped, her voice more of a wail of despair than anything. "Just tell me."

The two looked at each other. Doctor Perrez opened her mouth to speak, closed it, and then finally said.

"To be perfectly honest, with the technology we have here, either route is as dangerous as the other. That's the God's-honest truth."

Celia laughed. *God.* What a word to use in this situation.

"When can I see him?"

"Well," Perrez said, brightening up. "He's still in a bit of a narcotic haze but he's been asking after you. You should be able to see him around three o'clock. He may not be conscious though."

Celia prodded her egg and avocado wrap with her fork. Faced with the imminence of it, she wasn't even sure if she wanted to see him in his current condition. But he wanted to see her. She had to do it.

"Three o'clock. Sounds good," she whispered, and began to eat. The pesto almond bread exploded flavour onto her tongue and before she knew it she had an entire slice of it devoured.

"And how have you been settling in?" Sam asked her, chuckling. "No strange dreams or anything like that? No visions?"

"Pardon?" She asked, her mouth only a little full of almond bread.

"Oh, that must have been an odd question out of context. Do tell me one thing before I explain though, if you wouldn't mind— how did the landscape on the drive up make you feel?"

"Well," answered Celia, though she didn't know why she was acquiescing to such strange questions. "It made me feel tiny, almost dizzy or something. It was kind of overwhelming actually."

"Yes," Sam said, almost purred, he sounded so satisfied. "This island is famous for the effect the landscape has on people. It's something similar to Jerusalem or Montsegur Syndrome. It can impress upon people so much that sometimes they start seeing things, or believing they're receiving prophecies in their dreams."

"Well I haven't had any odd dreams," Celia said, and at least that part was true.

"Coming here made me reconsider my atheism," Janet laughed through a mouthful of toast. "The way I was affected by this place. I ended up getting involved with the local church. My grandmother would be proud."

"I never got anything like that myself, unfortunately," Sam said. "It sounds fascinating."

Could this explain what's been happening to me? Celia thought. *No, it couldn't, it started before I came here. Hadn't it?*

Or was that her mind playing tricks on her?

"That's why this place is called Inishee after all." Sam said. "Inish Sidhe. Isle of The Sidhe, the neighbours. The good people."

"I don't understand," Celia said.

"Fairies, of course," Janet said with a wink and an eye roll.

"Well it's bad luck to say that one," Sam said, wrinkling his nose. "Not that someone who works in a hospital should believe in such things. It's just interesting. Nobody knows what causes a location to have such intense psychological effects on people. In the past people would have classed it up to the place being a holy site, or a dwelling place of . . . other beings."

Celia didn't know how to respond. She took a big drink of her coffee. It was hot and dark and exquisite. She sighed as the caffeine surged through her body.

"Time to shut up, Sam," Sam said to himself, his voice tinged with humour

They ate a while in silence, sipped tea and coffee, letting the ambient murmur of other people's chatter roll over them.

There was a sickness in the room they all could feel but nobody wanted to mention.

Janet winced, and it seemed to take an enormous amount of difficulty for her to swallow the first mouthful of her porridge.

You've felt it too, those new moon moments where the lights go up and the magic ends and the bar room floor is covered in sticky disgusting shit that somebody else has to clean. The pores of your face in high definition.

"Are you okay?" Celia asked.

"This milk is gone off. Oh my God that was horrible."

"Should have just spat it back in the bowl," Celia said wryly.

The sludge pushing slowly through your intestines right now. Your heart could cease to beat at any minute, and then you will belong to us forever.

"Felt inappropriate." Janet pushed the bowl away.

Celia was glad to have taken her coffee black.

"Oh, dear, well it's inappropriate to poison yourself in the name of manners," Sam said, looking concerned.

"That's my appetite ruined." Janet sighed. "Every day here there seems to be something or another past its expiration date. I don't know how they keep managing to fuck that up."

And it is we that govern the sleep of the injured, we who crawl across the skin toward the open wound. Toward the tendency inside you to hurt others. We have orchestrated your every betrayal.

"Global supply issues maybe," Sam suggested.

"Say, Celia," Janet's tone brightened. "Since you and I both have some time now, and we're set to go see Martin later, how about you accompany me to the gallery to see the unveiling of the new piece?"

Celia's mind returned to that sunlit room, the painting of the guitar player by firelight.

Futile SCRIBBLINGS of SHIT APE SHIT ON DEAD GOD SKIN, SLAUGHTER APE NO MEANING FUCK APE RETCHPISS RETCH

"Ah, sure why not." She responded. "Sounds nice."

THERE IS NOTHING

Patient is slipping, administer shock?
No. Allow it.
Good. This is good.
Tell me what you see.

Slide 6b:

conidiosporic mitosis

Everything was covered in black mould. The walls were textured like a rotting orange, and the floor varied from stained tile to organic mush that threatened to devour Martin's feet as he moved forward. Every door he passed was open, and overfull with the tangled frames of beds.

"Please . . . " A parched voice drifted through the acrid air.

Martin opened his mouth to speak, but thought twice. At the thought of being silent, his lungs started to tickle. Shouldn't he be coughing to keep the spores out? Wouldn't that feel better? A rattling moan came from ahead of him, or was it from within one of those rooms of tangled metal and mildew-ravaged sheets? The sound sent such a visceral thrill through his spine that he stumbled, his hand landing in a bowl of stagnant fluid atop an abandoned cart.

"Gakh!" He cried.

"Somebody?" The voice said, audible with ragged hope. "Please . . . They said . . . It wouldn't be long.. I need a bed. It hurts I need . . . a bed."

Martin let himself cough. He decided that the voice must have been coming from just around the corner up ahead. There was a worn sign on the wall that indicated a stairwell. His mind conjured a papery old man strapped to a trolley, abandoned by long dead staff to die in the halls. Certainly he'd heard stories of such things happening all the time with how backed up the healthcare system was, but this mould-eaten hellhole struck him as, well, not exactly real.

He pressed forward, remembering his prayer on the way out

of his room. Whoever he was about to encounter, their meeting was fated. As he approached the corner, he started to get warm, then hot, sweat pouring down his body, making his gown stick to his skin, and itch. Was something happening with his body? Some complication in his condition?

The smell hit him next, slicing through the mouldy air like a blade. Burning hair, cooking meat. He was about to step into an oven. He hesitated at the very lip of the corner, another ward ahead of him stuffed with piled and rotting hospital junk, faint twilight from a window shining through the gaps in the detritus.

"Please . . . It hurtss . . . "

A crackling, crunching sound from behind him, the other end of the hallway, like glass underfoot.

"Missterrr Cammmpbelllll." A voice came from behind him. Trim and warm and British sounding, but too low pitched, too slow to be anything other than the denizen of a nightmare.

More crackling, more crunching coming closer, the crunches too close together for the person to be running, too fast to be walking, crunch crunch crunch crunch crunch.

Martin launched himself into the heat, grabbing for the rail of the stairs, wincing from the temperature, trying not to lose balance on the metal grating of the steps. Instead of walls, there were slats of tin, nailed skitter-skatter to give an impression of a boundary between the stairwell and the furnace beyond, with skins, some tanned, some dripping, stretched between the pipes. No, not just skins, Martin could make out warped hands, fingernails, teeth here and there, like human forms had been fed through a mincer without shredding, just stretched, warping, the bones melding into the muscles, into the skin.

"Returntoyourroommistercampbell" A woman's voice. A stern, schoolteacher's voice sped up just beyond what was right.

Martin stumbled onto the landing, back to linoleum and grey twilight but still the heat, still the skin-things leering down at him from the stairwell, and the trolley sitting there was empty, clean and white save for a patch of dark red stain where a patient's stomach would be, and a gummy pink wad of flesh, an ulcer freed from its victim.

Another crack from behind him, this one vertebral, organic, and Martin didn't stop, he moved as fast as he could without making himself trip and fall, his mismatched limbs struggling to support his weight, his heart thudding.

But as he crossed the second corner, he glanced back before he could stop himself.

There were four of them, uniforms encrusted in filth and gore, and their faces were made featureless by the yellow biohazard bags pulled tight over their heads. Their sleeves and aprons dripped with something, maybe dust—if dust could writhe, if dust was segmented and had too many legs. Two of them had shining instruments he couldn't identify—barbed and bladed and convoluted. The one closest to him held a mouldering chart aloft with two hands, which itself writhed just under the surface, and he could have sworn that the one the furthest from him had its hands under its apron, caressing itself beneath the material.

Of course, Martin screamed.

The stairs lead down into darkness. He kept moving across slick linoleum, bumping up against beds, gripping at hanging rubber tubing, collapsed light fixtures.

"I wanna go home," someone choked nearby.

The sound of heart monitors, respirators. Darkness. He bumped painfully into something, a wall—a door. It was heavy, but it moved, opening; electric white light streaming in.

No, they'll see you.
Without eyes they'll see you.
Without souls they'll drag you away.
And you'll be his, forever.

The room was small; a concrete box with a tall, nakedly bulbed lamp, a dental chair with a human figure wrapped in gauze lying bound to it with leather straps, and a heavy looking metal wash station.

"Jill?" He whispered to the figure.

The door behind him moved, scraping on the concrete floor.

Martin lurched toward the wash station and went around the far side of it, never taking his eyes off the door, watching a pale and blood-soaked figure in bleached scrubs creep its way in, one bandaged hand around the lip of the door, moving silently as if in slow motion. He pushed the wash station with all his strength, feeling his vertebrae click, his abdomen stretch to breaking point. Whatever connection it had to the wall broke, black sludge spattering onto the cold floor, and Martin heaved, shoving the station toward the door.

He shoved it hard against the figure, and he swiped at it with a fist, hitting its plastic-wrapped head, feeling thick liquid contents shifting inside. The grotesquerie receded like a mist, and he threw everything he had into getting the wash-station flush against the wall.

He knew it wouldn't be enough, but it was all the fight he had in him. He slumped down against the cold metal, his body aching all over, when a muffled voice came from the figure behind him.

Muffled, but still recognisable.

"Martin?"

Try to breathe, go back, go back
To the screen. Good.
I know it hurts, that's good.
It means your blood is still moving in there.
To the screen.
How did Celia get into the basement?
How did she get on the other side of the walls?

Dr. Bethany McGuire, MD:
Testimony II

I woke up at 5am this morning, screaming. It was the war again. The feeling of the genocidal maniacs closing in on us, knowing that the most beautiful people I would ever meet were about to meet more brutal ends than anyone but their perpetrators deserved.

I wish I had died there.

I feel like I recognise their faces sometimes, in the halls. Like. Sometimes I think I recognise soldiers I saw back then. The kind of soldiers that pulled the plug on babies and burned families alive. Retiring all happy and peaceful, handed jobs where they can take care of the vulnerable.

Makes me . . . Makes me feel . . .

(Doctor McGuire makes a guttering grunting sound before steadying her breathing and continuing)

I found two nurses today laughing at a patient who's got this condition that makes their facial muscles all fuse together into one painful hypertense slab of gristle. They were just standing there and laughing as the patient projectile vomited onto her own sheets. I tried to intervene, but Dr. Harcourt explained to me that this was just part of our patient's

Valkyrie Loughcrewe

treatment. He has the voice and eyes of a lizard.

The thing I didn't realise at the time was that when the nurses weren't laughing, the patient wasn't vomiting. This is the most direct evidence of mistreatment that I've found so far. I'm guilty to admit it, but I'm excited. Maybe now, we can . . .

. . . Fuck, that sounded bad. I need to redo this.

(end of recording)

Slide 6c:

Stendhaloidal Haemmorhagic Beatitude:
Praxis

Celia stepped into the conservatory, marvelling at the ceramics and sculpture work on plinths before the wall of portraits. Her eyes passed over a small sculpture of what looked to be a mother and child, made of porcelain with swirls of colour through it that accentuated the sense of movement of the piece, the mother swinging her baby in her arms, both rapt with the joy of motion and existence. The innocent beauty of the piece made her chest heave with sorrow, and she crushed the feeling with a ragged breath.

Eyes drifting to another painting, along the wall,
tall and thin, a dusty wasteland, jagged and inhospitable
like Celia, a place where the stuff of life goes to die.
Grey and dry, but her wish came true
Forced into flesh
Martin
Another crushed feeling, mental membranes throbbing faster,
Another painting, another psychic impalement,
A human figure formed from the grey rubble of the wasteland,
Head, chest, abdomen hollow, bright waters pouring in and
through the body.
She was projecting, the image was benign,
Conveying healing, but it hurt her to see
Martin's body hollowed out and reconfigured
I should turn around but my eyes
Behind my eyes throbbing, hurting
Drifting to the final image in the triptych.

Valkyrie Loughcrewe

Celia felt a hand on her shoulder. She shuddered, but didn't shriek, only letting out a confused bleat, like a wounded exhausted animal. She realised then how loud she had been struggling for breath, for grounding.

"Madam, are you alright?" A soft voice.

Her unfocused eyes stared ahead, pointed at the painting of an androgynous figure skipping through a newly grown forest, toward a rising (or setting?) sun. Celia faced the source of the concerned voice. The first thing she noticed was the eyepatch, the short crop of hedgehog sharp golden-brown hair, the weathered, angular face. The slight smile peering out behind his concerned gaze and furrowed brow.

"Do you need to step outside?"

The second thing she noticed was the painting, the new painting, freshly unveiled. That was when her nose began to bleed, and the world of sanity slipped away entirely, into an entirely abstract image, tiles of different colours and textures in crisscrossing intimate detail—fragments of sub-patterns without resolution, no greater vision outside of the tiny, swarming intricacies. Oil and acrylic and watercolour, gold-leaf and marker, pencil and charcoal, colour and shade.

The singular, maddening focal point, the one solidly intentional stroke, was a great slash down the centre of the piece, cleaving the maelstrom of chaotic interlocking, unresolving patterns, in two.

> *Brace the patient for sudden haemorrhaging.*
> *We need to pivot here.*
> *Trigger-phrase "Eidolon"*
> *Invert.*
> *Now.*

"Jill?"

An overwhelming smell of fabric, her face irritated, scratchy, and a bleary obstruction over her eyes. She tried to breathe, and felt cotton on her tongue. She tried to move but couldn't. She wondered if she was dreaming.

Someone was crying. It was a weeping Celia had only ever

heard at a distance, through a locked door, through a window at night.

"Martin?" She said aloud, her voice muffled by whatever it was that covered her face.

Within an instant, she felt tremulous hands pulling at the fabric around her face, unwrapping it—bandages, she could see, and as her vision cleared—there he was. Pale and sweating, bags under his eyes; Martin.

"You can't be real," he said, his voice sounding parched. "Please, just get it over with, turn into whatever you really are. I'm not fooled this time."

Martin staggered back against the desk. Celia knew she was dreaming then, for he was in the same clothes he had worn that night, the night her life became a nightmare. Brown coat, white shirt, black tie, grey slacks. His body was as it had been, far from the twisted horror she had expected. She looked down, seeing through the searing light of the naked bulb to her right, that her body was strapped to some kind of chair, wrapped head to toe in bandages, though everything but her face felt completely numb.

"This is a dream," she said to herself.

"Oh is it?" Martin laughed, slumping down to the floor. "I suppose you're standing by my bedside telling me that I need to wake up. It's all that simple is it? I crashed the car or something, and I'm in a coma? Hell, maybe you're dead. Maybe I killed you with my idiotic driving. Probably was looking at my phone and sent us off a cliff, didn't I?"

Of all the things that could have brought Celia to her end, Martin thought, of all the catastrophes she'd endured over her career, it would only be fitting that it would be him to finally do her in. Maybe he was in hell, being punished. It would be well deserved.

"Martin . . . I'm the one dreaming. You're . . . " She lost her words, her mind flashing through the horrors of that night.

"Dead?" Martin asked. "I need to know what's happening to me, Celia, I've been trapped in this nightmare of a hospital, I'm being tormented by . . . demons, I think. I need to get out somehow."

"The last thing I remember was stepping into a gallery at the hospital, and I saw this . . . painting, and everything started to get dim, and now I'm here," Celia said, her voice distant.

Valkyrie Loughcrewe

Her eyes drifted upward, and that was when she noticed that the room had no ceiling. She was looking up at the ceiling of a hospital corridor, at people drifting by, and she realised that she was being wheeled on a gurney through the corridors of the Bannican.

Something slammed against the door. Martin felt the desk shift with the impact as if it weighed about as much as a wooden shelf. It wasn't going to hold.

"Missssssterrrr Campbelllll . . . " Only Martin could hear the slowed down voice of the thing behind the door. "It'ssss tiiiiime forrr treeeeaaaatmennnnnt."

"They have me in a stretcher," Celia said dreamily.

"Celia," Martin said, standing, going to her. He gripped her arm. "Celia, you have to get out of this hospital. If you can, if you can get home, leave me. I'll find a way out. I think it's too late for you to save me. But you can tell the world, let them know, like you always do."

Celia's eyes snapped to his, before rolling back into her head.

"Won't . . . leave you . . . "

Something grabbed him from behind. Gloved hands gripping his hair, wrapping around his waist—causing him to go into a spasm of horror before he realised he wasn't feeling any pressure on the bulging belly the implanted womb had given him. He couldn't look down but he felt hands grabbing his arms, wrenching them back, and he felt that they were gripping the sleeves of a jacket, not the bare mismatched arms he had been forced to acclimatise to.

They dragged him away; the concrete room with the bandaged form of Celia getting smaller and smaller until the light went out. Then the water hit. Martin found himself plunging into freezing black water in darkness, his ears filling with a sound of thunderous violence as he was held down in a rushing flood. Though his mind had decided on this being little more than just a dream, his all too physical body hadn't, and he held his breath, struggling against that which held him.

He thought he had known darkness before, but his vision darkened still as his lungs burned for breath, and in the moment before he finally gasped, he was pushed forward, his head breaking the surface. The lights blinked on, halogen strips barely clinging to the fissured ceiling.

He sat up, his body once again heaving with the changes forced upon it. The building groaned around him. The doors to the ward he was in were blocked by rubble, and the room was different to the one he had woken up in twice before. White walls. Signs in some kind of Asian script. The water was grey, and it stank, and he could hear people shouting urgently in the distance, howls of pain, crying children. Martin felt like he had seen this, or something like it, before. A blurry, shaky video on his social media timeline, or on the news. One of Celia's stories. Catastrophic flooding somewhere in the world. Somewhere else.

He felt a sharp pain in his hand and tried to withdraw it, but it was weighed down. He looked to find a huge, hairless rat gnawing on the flesh between his forefinger and thumb, gnarled fingers wrapped around the side of the gurney he was sitting on. Martin screamed and pulled hard, and his hand came free along with a strip of his flesh. The water bubbled around him, and more rats crawled over him. They were more monstrous than any animal he'd ever seen, like the suggestion of rats carved from bloated, dead flesh.

Martin shrieked and batted at the things as they crawled up out of the water, grabbing at him with their tiny crooked paws, gnashing with lopsided jaws. The wound on his hand burned even worse every time his hand made contact with their clammy skin.

The lights blinked. Once, twice, a rat-thing getting purchase on him, wriggling its way up the inside of his shirt, three times—and they went out. He screamed, involuntarily throwing himself off the gurney into the foetid waist deep floodwater. The rat inside his shirt gripped him hard, tiny needle claws cutting through skin as his shirt took water, and he grabbed at it, squeezed it as he waded away from the other rats in a vain attempt to escape them.

A choir of high-pitched screams in the dark. Something cold and spindly shooting up from the water, under his shirt, across his chest, and ripping the creature away, its nails raking shallow gouges down his abdomen.

The lights came up, a throb, the walls were no longer white, the water no longer grey, or cold. A grating, alien voice spoke, dry and scratchy, like the chittering of insects.

Valkyrie Loughcrewe

> *This place wants to devour you.*
> *He tried to keep you safe and comfortable.*
> *But of course you had to fight him*
> *Well, you'll have to keep fighting now,*
> *Though your chances of being saved*
> *are getting lower with every passing second.*

A great fleshy thing hung before him like a fruit, a ring of foetal tissue, a ring of developing faces and vestigial hands and feet, like a human pumpkin growing from a singular umbilical cord which descended from infinity. The amniotic fluid he stood in was warm, and it was tempting to lie back and float in it. Another voice came, this one familiar, warm, but he couldn't quite pace it.

> *I will keep you safe,*
> *Protect you from the nightmares*

The voices which spoke to him seemed to come from the other side of the great hanging thing, and if Martin squinted, he could just about make out a blurry shadow-figure at the very edges of his vision.

> *That's it. Lie back.*
> *Forget.*
> *Drift away, and let it all happen.*

Martin's eyelids felt heavy, and the fluid was so very warm, the pain of his wounds already beginning to flow out of him, an invisible current running down his body and into the fluid. He let his knees go soft, crouching down a little, and the warmth felt so good rising up across his body.

He lay back, and that was when he realised where he knew the voice from. The fogged pane of glass, the blurry shape which muttered to himself as he worked on carving up flesh and bone. The doctor. The doctor who did this to him. The spring-loaded restraints on the steel frame which lay just beneath the surface triggered, their barbs tearing into his skin, hooking into cartilage and bone before dragging him down into the murk.

Puppet's Banquet

It will all be over soon.
She just needs to wake up
and set us all free.

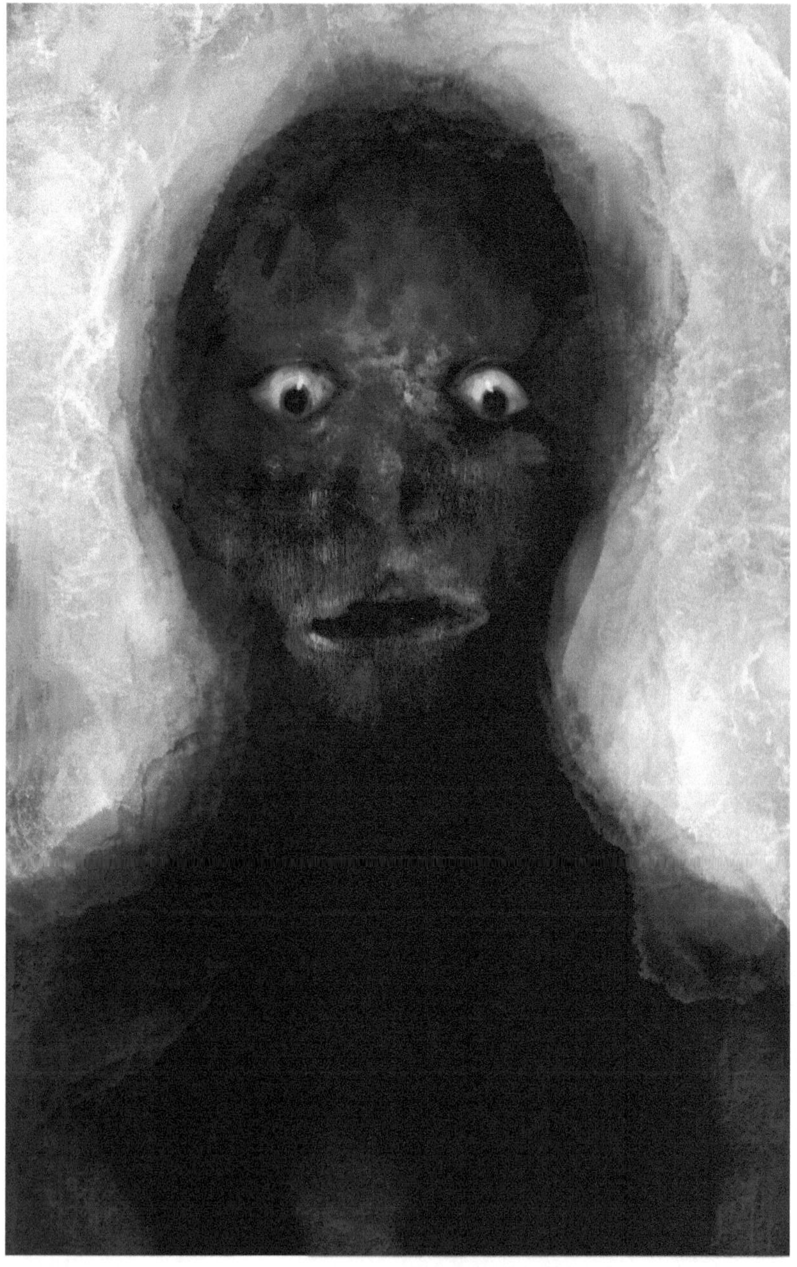

Slide 7:

Ambiguous Flaws in the
Pseudorevelatory Perceptive

Celia came back to consciousness slowly, intermittently, her nose picking up the scent of the perfumed room she had been allocated at the hospital, her body feeling the snug embrace of the heavy blankets, returning to sleep, to oblivion, until eventually her mind began to piece it all together. The hospital, her madness, the gallery, the painting, the dream. Martin.

She sat, feeling the tug of an intravenous drip in her arm. Her vision was blurry, and a figure rushed from sitting unseen in the corner to pushing her back down into the softness of the bed.

"Oh, no no no, Mrs. Campbell, you've just suffered quite the brain haemorrhage. You shouldn't even be sitting up."

"Muhmnuhm." Celia slurred. "Khee Mumhnun."

"You're lucky you were here when this happened. You had a clot in your brain that was like a ticking time bomb. You're going to have to spend significant time to recover here, Celia. We've called your family and they've arranged to pay for everything. By the time you're recovered, Martin should be too. Just sit tight, Celia. We have you now."

My family? She thought in darkness as sleep returned to her body. *What family? The husk of my father? My estranged cousins? Did they mean Martin's family?*

It was so dark by the time she regained consciousness again that the only indication she was even awake was the muffled crash of distant waves. She rolled over with a groan and reached out for her bedside locker, her body forgetting where it was, but nonetheless she found a flat wooden surface, and on it, her phone. The IV drip was no longer in her arm. She wondered how much time had passed.

A blood clot, a blood clot that would have killed her. That must have explained the hallucinations. That would make this whole horrific series of events into more of a twisted miracle, the pair of them guided by fate to a time and place where she could be saved from an event that would have otherwise ended her life. She felt guilty for even having that thought. The obscenity of the horror that Martin had suffered, was still suffering from, was hardly a fair price for such a miracle. Beyond all of that even still, there was something else gnawing at her mind.

The painting. Though she had been overwhelmed by the entire gallery, even in a way that could have indicated that she was building to a haemorrhage unrelated to where she was, she couldn't shake the fact that somehow it had been the painting that had caused it. In the moment where Celia had locked eyes on the thing, it had spoken to her as if she had just read her own name written in an alien language, as if she had just picked a familiar face from a crowd, the face of someone she never wanted to see. It was as if it had been waiting for her, and her for it, and the pain of that recognition had hurt so acutely it almost tore her brain apart from the inside out.

The searing white boot-up screen of her phone assailed her eyes, and her heart leapt for a moment, expecting an orderly to loom out of the darkness and take it from her. No such thing happened, and the phone came active in earnest. The date was two days after she saw the painting, three after she had first checked in to the Bannican.

She hopped onto the internet and searched for the Bannican institute. There was nothing. An ancestry article for the surname Bannican, something called "the crossmaglen conspiracy" which seemed to involve Irish republican schoolteachers in the 1800s, one of whom was named Bannican, and there was a science article on a new type Lof bacteria by the name of Bannicus in China. She even looked the place up on the maps app just in case the search engine had missed something.

There was no trace of it. But hadn't she followed the GPS there on the way up? Or had she just set a course for the ferry she was meant to catch that day? Her memories felt so hazy and scrambled. Absent-mindedly she typed in "Bannican art gallery" to the search.

Her breath caught when she saw that the first result was from a business networking site, from the profile of a Doctor Millard Whitehead. The sight of the name of the man who had accosted her that night–who had stolen her husband from her and put him through so much torment–caused her body to convulse.

She threw the phone on the bed. The faint light emanating from it illuminated her room, a ghostly pale outline of itself, its antiquated furniture and the spaciousness of its shadows feeling all too haunted, all too pregnant with potential lurking presence.

She reached for the lamp and lit the place fully. It felt a little less threatening, though the looming emptiness of the armoire and ensuite bathroom still sucked like a void in her subconscious. She sat up fully, reached for the phone and picked it up again, brought herself to look again at the search results. The main header of the result simply displayed the name Dr. Millard Whitehead, MD, and the name of the site, and below that was an excerpt from the post she had called up. It was just a series of hashtags.

#jung #arttherapy #postmodern #bannican #gallery #mentalhealth #redbook

Celia tapped into the link, her breath shallow, and the post loaded: a single image of a great canvas in a studio with beige walls and polished oak floorboards. On the canvas was an unfinished painting— *the* painting. She threw the phone again, and this time it slipped off the end of the bed, dropping to the carpeted floor with a dull thump.

Her breathing got harsher and harsher, as fear and anger intermingled within her blood. This wasn't a coincidence. This wasn't a tragedy. It was a game, it was a nightmare. It was torture. Someone had taken Celia and her husband out of their lives and placed them into a nightmare.

She turned, letting her legs hang off the side of the bed, and with a scurrying wave of revulsion she realised that she was wearing a white silken nightgown, one that she absolutely had not put herself into. The idea of someone else taking her clothes off– seeing her naked, redressing her while she was unconscious–made her want to scream, made her feel so horrifically vulnerable that her body immediately erupted with tremors.

Valkyrie Loughcrewe

So tiny, just clinging to a little rock in a sea of darkness, roiling and crashing against the jagged edges of safety. Your tormenter is the air itself, the black of every shadow. Only he knows what he did, and you only know the result of his actions. Best- case scenario, the details slowly trickle out of the gibbering mouth of your ruined lover as he reveals them drop by drop, a rich dark wine, over the years, until it creates a flood to drown the pair of you.
Worst case- you get your chance to experience them firsthand, when your tormenter reaches his pale hand down from the night sky and snatches you away, at the cruellest possible moment.

The thing inside her was hysteria, screaming and wailing, a beast to set her upon a track of panophobia. The simplest course of action—complete and utter helpless insanity. It clawed at her insides to get out of her mouth, and she shoved it down with the anger that had sparked a moment ago, with this newfound fledgling sense that this was not what she deserved, that there had to be something she could do, even if all it would amount to would be making an unholy mess. It felt so alien to the person she knew she was, but so darkly familiar all the same.

She breathed the tremors away, a battle in every inhale, a victory with every exhale.

She should leave. Reject this whole situation, get in the car, get the ferry, leave the island. If they fixed Martin, great, if they didn't, she would survive. Maybe that would be better, something new, something fresh.

She thought of the dream then, how afraid he was, how determined he was to escape the horror he was trapped in, and she felt guilt. But even in the dream, he had told her to leave, hadn't he?

It's too late to save me.

Stop standing there, Celia, do something. *I can't go out like this, I need to . . . Where did they put my clothes? All I can find are these stodgy slacks and sweaters from the seventies. Who's wardrobe is this even?*

She had to see him again, see whatever state they had him in. It wouldn't be enough to run. Nothing felt stable anymore, the walls, the inverted world behind the mirror, the layout of her own house. Even if he came back to her, would she wonder if it was really him? Would she still think herself as being stuck in this hospital, on this island? What would her dreams tell her?

She had to see, she thought, and then she could leave. To see Martin broken and twisted, in a hospital bed, in a dark ward, would at least give her some kind of clue about what was real and what wasn't. Afterward, therapy and medication would sort out the rest.

Another deep breath. Yes. That made just about enough sense to spur Celia into action.

She dressed with her eyes closed, a scratchy fleece over a thin sweatshirt that gave her an unpleasant stinging, pulling sensation as it dragged over her bare chest. She didn't want to think about what that was. She climbed into a pair of slightly too tight bellbottom jeans and was ready to go.

She pushed the door open, a gust of cold air meeting her. The corridor that led from her bedroom back down to the fourth floor of the hospital looked eerily still in the cobalt light of her phone's torch. There was a light switch on the wall, but she was afraid to touch it.

Maybe they'd know. Maybe the little metal panel would collapse into the wall as through the skin of a rotten fruit, and the dark ocean would rush in, its equilibrium broken, the entire hospital collapsing to explosive decompression. Wishful thinking.

Patient is struggling.
Agitated? Why?
Can you resonate with a part of what she's feeling?
Or is this a result of your current condition?
I want to keep you somewhat lucid, please, stop struggling for a moment,
And then we'll see what we can do with regards to medication again.
For now, just watch.
Just breathe. Focus on the screen. Respond, react. Your opinion is important to us.

Valkyrie Loughcrewe

Celia crept into the halls of the fourth floor, which were, mercifully, softly lit by orchid-shaped lamps along burgundy-coloured walls. The doors of one of the rooms along the hall opened, and a pair of orderlies guided out a moaning patient. She was tempted to hide, but simply stood transfixed at the sight of a seven-foot-tall shuffling mound of a thing stooping to get through the door.

It was dressed in a billowing blue, papery gown, and its head was shrouded with a white blanket. Most unsettlingly, it seemed to have a large protrusion emerging from its side which required its own wheelchair to manoeuvre, and even though it too was covered up, Celia could see hints of bulging grey flesh shot through with spidery blue veins.

Immediately, Celia doubted her sanity. There was no way that thing could get down a stairwell, nor had she seen any sort of lift that could fit its bulk. It was possible that they could carefully get it down the wide central stairs in the main hall of the building, but why even house a creature like that on the fourth floor?

The orderlies didn't even look at her. As she watched them move the moaning beast away, she began to wonder where she was even going. Where were they keeping Martin again? Christ, someone had told her, and she couldn't remember.

Room 3C of the West wing, or something? Had the guy even specified the floor number? He had definitely said something C, hadn't he? What wing was she even in now?

She moved over to the little metal plaque that hung next to the room the behemoth had lumbered out of:

A9
Summer Foxall
J.D. 1964 Cairo

Letter A, and the stairs to the little area with her room seemed to be at an extreme corner of the building. If she were to just follow this corridor around, maybe she could reach the C ward, and then it would just be a matter of finding the right floor, the right name. Her breathing was normalising now. The orderlies hadn't seen her, but after witnessing them, despite the disturbing appearance of their patient, she remembered where she was. It was a hospital, not a prison. She could roam freely if she wanted, so long as she didn't cause any trouble, right?

In the haze of her thoughts, she took the first staircase she found, absent-mindedly beginning to descend it instead of continuing her circuit around the wards, and there she ran into Sam.

He was with a doctor she recognised from somewhere, one with short hair and, of all things, an eye-patch. They looked surprised at first to see her, not moving aside to let her pass. Sam had a slight smile on his face, and the doctor with the eyepatch—good lord, his name badge read *Bannican*—his face was stony, his single green eye studying her.

Sam tilted his head and did a strange gesture with his right hand, splitting his fingers into pairs and crossing them around each other. A signal?

"Are you lucid?" He asked. "Are you . . . ?"

The second, unfinished question almost seemed like he was prompting her to finish his sentence.

"I'm . . . I—" Celia stammered.

"Celia," Sam said, his voice cold and hard, tinged with disappointment. "You've had a bad shock, you should be in bed, it's dangerous for you."

Celia started to step back up the staircase, and Sam approached her, cautiously.

When she hit the top step she broke into a run. Not in the direction of her room, of course not. She continued the circuit, looking for the next stairwell. She expected yelling, alarms being raised, orderlies pouring out of every shadow to restrain her, shove needles in her, send her back to Martin in the nightmare she had met him in. That would have at least felt like something that should have happened in an active, living and breathing world, instead all she could hear was soft panting breathing and running footsteps on carpet behind her, as Sam gave silent chase.

She beat him around the first corner, to the first stairwell, and decided to keep moving past it, to take a chance with a doorway. She thought he might get confused and race down the stairs, but she wasn't fast enough. The door was too heavy, it took her a second and a half to get through, hearing him gaining on her, expecting his hand to suddenly reach forward and grab her through her scratchy layers.

Valkyrie Loughcrewe

The door closed even slower behind her, and she found herself on a wooden mezzanine, a sort of library nook to her left, and a little wooden stair down to a dimly lit conservatory area overlooking a dark courtyard. She took the stairs. It was steep and slippery in the cold, and she fell down the second set, landing painfully on the cold polished wood below.

"Celia." Sam's voice was cold as he came through the door. "You're risking another haemorrhage."

She wanted to call out to her bizarre pursuer, the man who had decided to make her presence in the hospital his own personal concern since the moment she arrived.

What do you want from me? Why is there a painting from Millard Whitehead in your gallery? Why doesn't anything feel real anymore?

She stayed silent and pulled herself forward. There were a few ways she could have gone—out into the courtyard, into another hall through a pair of double doors, into a side room near the courtyard entrance, but close to here there was this metal door, like an industrial refrigerator door, covered in yellow warning signs, and it was ajar. She went for it, slipping through the gap, pulling it behind her, fearful of a squeak or a scrape or a whine, but it was silent, and she heard Sam descend the stairs and stand stock still for a moment.

Celia looked at what was in front of her, dingy, stone-walled stairs leading downward, lit by bare, flickering bulbs. The stairs went very far down, further than she could immediately see, each bulb running dimmer and dimmer, until only darkness remained to greet her.

A floorboard creaked outside the door. Another. Tentative footsteps toward the way she had entered.

"Celia." A sudden, raspy whisper from outside. "You've made a big mistake."

One more step, and Celia made a move, one step back onto the metal stairs, then another, and another, momentum building, she turned and faced the darkness.

Slide 7b:

Butcher's Meat

Pharmakos, the ritual of human sacrifice in ancient Greece, the idea that for to resolve a disaster in the community, one human being must be made to represent the entire tribe, and their encroaching doom must be resolved within that singular life, which of course in the process of resolution, brings that life to its end.

Suffice to say, as a Doctor, this is not a practice I should condone.

A pulsing, too much blood to the head. An ocean of torn plastic, yellow, marred red-brown, spilling foetid offal and rusted needles. Indistinct pale writhing in the mass, a pulsing, maggots in the meat, amid corroded obelisks, stretching into a choked horizon.

A weeping, like the crashing of the tide, and above it all, the warm, authorial voice of a man over crackling, warped speakers.

Pharmakon is the founding principle, the word meaning both cure and poison. The venom of the serpents which entwine the asclepius. In the deepest pits of suffering, in the blackest sulphurous pits which reject all life, lies the most potent panacea.

A shimmering, of nerves switching on and off, a message of agony firing at random throughout Martin's suspended body. Stars in an anthropomorphic constellation blinking in and out of existence.

Just as every revolution necessitates violence, all personal understanding and growth requires pain. The more intense the

Valkyrie Loughcrewe

suffering, the more holistic the development.
Like a hypnogogic flash, like a deathbed vision, an angel of
scalpels and bone saws, an iron maiden of intravenous tubing.
The pale face of Jill, staring outward, inverted, eyes raised,
lowered, into the pit of medical waste and corpses, of writhing
maggots, and the flies rising to meet her, descending from the
heavens of heaving toxic waste.
So it would seem to those in the deepest grips of despair, that
suicide would be the ultimate path to growth. The Panacea of
Self-Termination. But that is a delusion. The end of pain is the
end of potential.

Below her ribcage, a fossilised mass of porous strands, a pulsing in the tumour that blossomed all up the rusted cage of her entombment, wrapping around one of the corroded obelisks. Another crucified scapegoat in the expanse of wasted flesh.

But to die, and still suffer—to suffer the perdition of hell, as the
abrahamics attempted to obfuscate and corrupt—is not to be
punished. It is to be reborn.
It is rebirth. As the Western Child of Pharmakos, the Lion of
Israel, Christ Jesus was reborn.

A pulsing, in the ichneumon womb.

It is rebirth.

Slide 8:

Oparin-Haldane Syndrome

Some called him The Primordial.
Most called him Darwin.
Does that spark any recognition in you?
No, it doesn't seem to,
You're basically catatonic at this point, aren't you?
We're going to need to up your stimulants, i think.
Some painkillers too maybe, opiates.
Perhaps the patient is dissociating from the pain.
It is just so hard to medicate our way to a perfect, alert stillness.
A fundamental shame if there ever was one.

elia didn't know what to make of what she found down there, that dank chamber of concrete and metal, trailing wires all across the ground, marred steel tables covered in paperwork and ancient computers.

The glass containment tubes and their inhabitants, the dissected remains pinned in glass along the walls like abhorrent butterflies from some alien glade.

2014, Easter Island, October 31st. First Medical team found the patient in a cave behind a farmhouse. The cave, the surrounding structures and the immediate area had been overrun by micro and macro biological anomalies of classification bacteria, virus, and genii acari, phyla, fungi, arthropoda, hybrid, and unknown. Containment procedures were successful, no contamination. All invasive lifeforms seemed to die off beyond an 8 mile radius of the patient.

Valkyrie Loughcrewe

She walked among shelves of jars of caviar-like jellies, of the hollow, popcorn-like skins of dead lifeforms. A great vat of worms of all shapes, sizes and colours, crawling in a nutrient slime, hooked up to computers reading out acid green statistics she could not fathom.

2014, Easter Island. November 3. Analysis showed that every body fluid—from tears, sweat and saliva to waste product, including urine and faeces—spontaneously generates simple lifeforms, most commonly mites of novel species, previously unencountered nematodes, and phylae. Tumours on the body seem to indicate more complex biological constructs gestating in the patient's pores. A total of 1056 tumours have been recorded thus far, and the amount of previously unencountered species, families, and even genus are becoming too much for our researchers to keep track of.

Along the walls, skins with spindly limbs, larger insectoid specimens, something resembling a horseshoe crab crossed with a bat, stretched out with tacks behind glass. Trays and trays of pieces of meat, petri dishes of what looked to be mould and fungi.

Celia became so morbidly curious that she didn't even notice her consciousness diverging, two Celias splitting off to cover more ground, to see more anomalous things—a tentacled and hairy blob suspended in fluid, with teeth lining its underside—to explore more of the room—a massive refrigerator style door locked by keycard in between two hazmat suit lockers—floating like a dream through the freak show.

2014, Easter Island. November 11. Team attempted to operate on a facial tumour on the patient, which split open to reveal a gestating life-form of cystoid agate integument composition. The bioform attached itself to one of the team's containment suits, seemingly in an attempt to feed, but could not pierce the material of the suit. Analysis of the bioform revealed it to be a massive single-celled organism not dissimilar to a bacterium. It was also found to be full of unknown viral loads. A joint decision from management has been made to contain and extract the patient and incinerate the surrounding area.

One Celia ran a hand across the white metal of the containment door, and noticed her fingers slipping through the surface as she pressed against it, the solid matter becoming as ephemeral as air at the slightest insistence. The other Celia found herself drawn to one of the tables covered in papers, screens, and analytical equipment. The space under it overflowed with cardboard boxes, which spilled out and up across a series of shelves next to it, all filled with similarly formatted papers—endless reports of new things that had crawled from the body of the Primordial.

The most recent paper sat beside a petri dish which contained a single gummy piece of pink flesh, and beside that there sat an electron microscope with an array of analytical devices. The paper was handwritten, and the thing that caught her eye was a letter, a number, a name.

Jill McEvoy
Ward 9C 2F

Had she heard Martin say the name *Jill* while she was wrapped up in gauze? C ward of the second floor, number 9. Maybe that was where he was. Why was this just sitting out for her to find? She felt like a puppet being jerked around from synchronicity to dark synchronicity at the behest of a power she couldn't understand. A power so subtle and cruel she could have mistaken it for her own subconscious will, bending reality to torture and mislead her.

The note read of womb tissue collected from that woman, from Jill, and how they prepared it for use in an experiment involving someone called Darwin. The Celia at the table didn't know what any of it meant, or so she told herself. The other Celia plunged her arm into the white metal door, and it felt like sliding into a hot bath.

Why not step forward? Why not take a look? Despite all of the hideous anomalies squirming and preserved around her, despite the surrounding evidence of vile experiments and crimes beyond what could even be considered malpractice, there was something almost nostalgic about the way she felt.

Something about that place felt like a childhood memory of home.

"Oh my God, you *are* down here."

She stepped through the door, phasing through it, and she was back on that staircase, back in the cold darkness, in one piece, one consciousness. A man was speaking to her, shining a light in her face, and she was cold. Freezing cold.

"Please, come with me, love. I'm not going to hurt you," the man spoke, moving the flashlight so it reflected off the metal steps, putting everything into a soft illumination.

It was the doctor with the eyepatch and the short fuzzy brown hair, Bannican himself.

"You can't be down there, it's all boiler machines and electrical boxes, you'll hurt yourself."

In the pit of her stomach, Celia felt hungry, like she hadn't had a meal all day, maybe longer. She wanted to open her mouth, to tell him that she knew what he was doing, that she'd seen his experiments, seen the hell lurking just beyond the facade of this fancy hospital, but to even begin to speak those words was a prospect so absurd that she just stood there and stammered like a child.

"My name is Sean Bannican, I'm the administrator of the hospital. Celia, I was actually hoping to speak with you about the Ichneum—about your husband on the day you had your haemorrhage incident. I'm very sorry that happened. Please, come with me. Let us take care of you."

"You . . . You sent h-him after me," she said, "I can't trust any of you."

"I understand if you're feeling threatened or confused, Celia. Would you like to see Martin? I can take you to him right now. He's not very far away at all."

She took a step back, back toward the darkness, toward that good feeling of home, with the worms and the dead things and the boy who sweats miracles.

"You really don't want to go down there, Mrs. Campbell, please, please come up with me, please put down the scalpel."

What scalpel? She thought, recognising the tightness in her balled fist, the sliver of sweat slick steel between the shaking bunched muscle, skin and fat. At the realisation, she yelped, and dropped the thing. Bannican barely contained himself from lurching forward as the blade clattered down the stairs.

"It didn't cut you, did it!?" He asked.

That was all the opportunity needed. He bustled at her, went to her side, put one hand on her back and with the other gripped her own hand softly. He guided her up the stairs. By this point, poor Celia was catatonic with disorientation. She just gave in, loosened her grip on her strings, let the puppeteer do its work.

His cologne was strong but unobtrusive, smooth, like his scent was polished somehow. It was oddly comforting.

"They really should have taken you to see your husband as soon as you arrived, I don't know what the hell they were thinking."

The compassion in his voice unsettled her. It sounded too genuine, not like someone trying to placate a lunatic that was endangering herself alongside the operation of his hospital. Why would he care so much about her? Nobody was that compassionate without a reason. It didn't make sense.

He let her go when they reached the top of the stairs, stepping back into that little atrium facing the darkness of the courtyard through glass.

"What happened to you two was one of the most absurdly horrific incidents that has ever brought someone through the doors of this building," he said, looking at her in the reflection.

She looked so haggard, standing next to his robust frame. So pale and ravaged by time.

"I can't undo the horrors that you and Martin have experienced, however I can make sure that you two are taken care of here. That can only be done with your cooperation, Celia. I'm ready to forget any of this happened, if you're willing to come with me to see your husband, and then return to your bed to get the rest you need. Can you do that, Celia?"

Staring at herself, into her own wide, dark, empty eyes, Celia nodded.

"Good," the doctor said, his voice tinged with sadness.

He raised a hand as if to pat Celia on the back, but lowered it again.

The ward they had Martin in was beautiful. Fully wood-panelled, with tall, ornate windows overlooking the sea. The sun was just beginning to rise, the first orange rays of day making the polished wood shine, making a mockery of the soft electric light's attempts to mimic the dawn's effortless glory.

Martin's misshapen body was largely hidden under his silky blankets. His head lay sideways on a large pillow, and his mouth was open, jaw slackened from the depth of the narcotic coma being trickled into his bloodstream by intravenous drip.

The patches of grey that had been starting to gnaw at the sides of his hairline were now in full bloom, ragged streaks that made their way all the way to the back of his skull. The heart monitor beeped away softly, his condition stable.

"Is he dreaming?" Celia asked.

"No, I wouldn't say so," Doctor Bannican responded. "This stuff tends to send patients into the void. He'll wake up good as new. It will have been no time at all for him."

"Was there someone else in this ward with him?"

An empty bed sat parallel to his, and there had been no name but Martin's on the plaque outside.

"Hm?" He sounded a little taken aback by the question. "Yes there was, a leukaemia patient. We had treated him before for an odd condition in his youth, and he decided to hospice here. He passed only last week."

So there was no Jill. Of course there hadn't been. It was the haemorrhage. It had all been the haemorrhage. Celia was starting to believe that maybe the condition Martin had been admitted for was something other than the Frankensteinian abomination that haunted her memory, although the tumorous bump under the sheet where Martin's belly should be didn't go away as she looked at it.

"I just want to forget about all this."

"Well, look," Doctor Bannican said, face glowing in the dawn light. "Someone's on their way up now to take you back to your room. They've got medicine to help you recover from the haemorrhage. You have a sleep, and we'll take this thing out of your husband, and you'll never have to think of it again. We'll run some tests to make sure you haven't got any lasting brain damage, and in about two weeks, you and your husband can go home."

Celia heard the door open behind her. Sean Bannican's face hardened somewhat, his single green eye studying her for something.

"Now you're sure there isn't anything else that's been troubling you?" He asked.

Celia felt a chill. Considering all the talk of forgetting and moving on, there was a sudden dissonance to the words that made her vision judder, her mind threatening to split again. Was he testing her? The look in his eyes seemed anything but malicious. He seemed pleading, almost. He looked to his side, to whoever was approaching, and opened his mouth as if to say something, but then he smiled.

"Sam will take you to your room," he said. "There should be a dinner there waiting for you there, too."

Celia walked quietly through the halls with the orderly as sunrise roused the bustle of the morning. He brought her to her room in the spire, and stood smiling vacantly as she entered. She took the pills she had been given with the still-warm food they had left for her, sank into her big comfortable bed, and she slept.

And she dreamt.

Dr. Bethany McGuire, MD:
Testimony III

The cattle are screaming, and the herders are as savage pagans, building a pyre of blackening bone and boiling blood. I think I understand it now, we've spent so much time as a species building our temples of healing, worshipping them and their priests as infallible sources of divinity, showering them with wealth, that they've become hollow. Flat. Two dimensional images. A white coat without a face.

What rules the temples when healing is no longer our goal? What are these shrines built in testament to? The sickness. They worship the sickness, they are avatars of the sickness. It bleeds through every pore. In the centre of man's domain it manifested as cruelty, psychopathy, torture and violation of the weak and innocent.

Here, at the edge of the world, the sickness isn't stopping at corrupting us from within. It's in the food. Everything on the shelves keeps spoiling now, they can't serve a decent meal without something blackened and slithering assaulting our tastebuds. Conversations in the halls barely resemble human speech, the dialect layers and layers of context removed from consensus reality.

The walls are crumbling. I can't just stand here any more and ramble into the void for

Valkyrie Loughcrewe

something, anyone, no one to help me. To stop them.

I have to stop them. I have to remove the sickness.

They made a fatal mistake bringing her here.

It can be me.

I can use her to prolapse their God and watch it unbirth into fucking wretched stench of-

(speech becomes unintelligible)

Slide 8b:

Geminae Umbra Syndrome

Celia sat in an uncomfortable metal chair, and there was a man sitting across from her, a skeletal man with naught but a napkin draped across his lap. His eyes were white, rolled back in their sockets; and a harsh stage light from above lit him unflatteringly, casting every wrinkle and pit in his body into stark shadows.

They were in a padded cell. The man had two shadows. His body was shrivelled with dehydration. They were in a padded cell, and Celia could feel flies landing on her skin, taking off again, landing again. She wanted to bat them away, but was stuck in that hazy drunken stupor of a half engaged dreamer.

The sun is setting on your final chance. The man said without speaking. *But the darkness has not yet taken hold. Leave this place immediately.*

Celia wet her parched lips with her tongue, and it briefly butted off an insect in flight. Revulsion pulsed through her body. Feeling came into her hands and feet. She looked down. She was back in the white nightgown.

They cannot complete their blasphemy without your hands to guide them.

The insects were crawling all over his body, all over Celia's skin. It was as if they had all come crawling out from hiding, large black segmented and winged things with barbed legs and chittering, mandibled heads. The shadows. They were crawling out of the shadows on the wall. Every passing moment more came flitting out

Valkyrie Loughcrewe

of the twin, man-shaped pools of darkness, flying in spirals, landing on warm flesh, gathering in crowds in the corners.

It was too much, it was time to wake up.

You need to listen, you need to run. There are two of you, but if you run you can prevent the dark one from completing her journey. You can keep him down there, beneath the hospital.

Celia stood, the cold of the floor on her soles shocking through her body. She batted away flies, pinched herself, scrunched her eyes tight, tried everything she could to wake up. The man with two shadows opened his mouth and spoke, in a rasping moaning voice.

"But . . . you . . . have . . . to . . . "

Celia backed up against the cold metal handle of a door. She grabbed it, pulled it, found the door unlocked.

"Run . . . "

Slide 9:

Effingo Vehemens Syndrome

She threw herself out of the cell, leaving the door open behind her. The hall was stark, and white, the floor linoleum tile, and soft daylight was coming in through an opaque, barred window. Somewhere in the distance she could hear voices shouting, slamming doors, knocking and banging of things being hurriedly rearranged.

Celia ran down the hall, feeling the chill of the floor running up her body, and she pushed through a double door, finding herself in a warmly lit, carpeted hall, in the Bannican. It still seemed to be early in the day, and there was definitely something wrong even apart from the fact that Celia had seemed to transition from dream to reality without waking up.

"Get Greenstein out of the garden and locked down before sounding any alarm!" Someone was barking orders nearby, their voice stressed to the point of breaking.

"We can't sound the alarm at all, Campbell is going into labour any moment, and we need to find Odessa first and foremost. That takes precedence. If you come across Melinda or Ibramovic, just take them out. Nothing else matters now."

Celia could hear murmurs of assent and disagreement, there was a door ajar, an office with a bronze plaque on the door. Celia tried to calm her breath, tried to will herself to wake up, and she walked backward, away from that office, unable to take her eyes off the half open door.

"She could be in the head office." A woman's voice.

"Oh, wishful thinking." Another woman's voice.

It was around that time that Celia decided that all of the things she had experienced urging her to just pick up and leave had been absolutely correct. She had no car keys, no jacket, not even any shoes, but it didn't seem to matter. She just needed to be out of that hospital, and as far away from it as possible. Any escape route would do. A fire escape, anything. There was nothing left within the walls of the Bannican but madness, nothing left to learn but whatever unforeseeable torment they ultimately had planned for her. That last vestige of solid ground was about to give way to the void, and the time had come to take a leap of faith or be surely consumed.

She was already in motion, she was already feeling the full body glow of the day on her skin, already pressing the bar of a door to the outside, fearing an alarm triggering upon tripping some unseen sensor, but no such alarm came.

Her eyes adjusted to the light, and her feet felt stone, and the first thing she noticed, which superseded the sight of the gardens, were the walls surrounding them. She wasn't out, she hadn't made it out—only into the courtyard, and there stood Sam.

But Sam wasn't looking at her, he was pleading with a figure she couldn't see, obscured by the tall water feature in the centre of the garden.

"That's it sir, just enjoy the garden, look at the lovely water. Our friends will be here soon to take you for tea, would you like that, sir?"

Celia turned back to the half open door, and leapt with fright as she saw a pair of wide eyed orderlies bearing down on her. She yelped, and slammed the door on them, and someone else yelped in reaction, startled by the loud noises. It was a dry, phlegmatic roar, and Sam screamed in terror—screamed *NO!*

Celia had no choice but to run toward him, around him, to some other door as the one behind her gave way to the weight of those on the other side. The orderlies yelled, not at her, but at the scene unfolding around the water feature. A crooked-backed old man with wispy white hair and a long white beard had come running out from behind the part of the water feature that obscured him, causing Sam to flinch, throw out his arms, his face a mask of primal terror.

The other doors and some windows into the courtyard had been opened, and the ten or so people in the process of pouring into the garden stopped and watched in horror as Leonid Abramovic, long term patient of the Bannican—and the first and only recorded case of Effingo Vehemens Syndrome—once again exhibited his special talent.

You know all about that, don't you?
You remember how it felt, when it happened to you?
It must have been such a profound agony,
especially considering your . . . special condition.

Celia didn't get much of a look at it, and part of her mind reeled to see the old man's hands seemingly plunge into Sam's torso, his face press much too far into Sam's chest, the skin seeming to pulse and stretch impossibly, blood rapidly spreading out to stain Sam's clothes, pour out of his mouth, his eyes rolling back into their sockets.

The other part of her mind said something to the effect of, *I've always wanted to see what that looks like. Let's stop and watch.*

A most fascinating condition indeed.
A strange sort of immune system symbiosis, reshaping the
entire body into,
how can I describe it in simple terms
Almost like the entire body functions like a giant white blood
cell which,
Upon encountering another life-form, reacts to it as if it were a threat.
The most remarkable quirk of this mutation however is that this
large,
Complex, multicellular facsimile of a single-celled organism
doesn't simply
eat
its prey.
It reshapes it, cell by cell into an exact clone of itself.
I do hope we can keep you alive long enough for you to describe
to me
Exactly how it felt to be transformed cell by screaming cell into
a withered
96-year-old man.
But first, I must conclude my thesis.

Valkyrie Loughcrewe

Celia did not stop, she ran through orchids and snapdragons, tearing up plants and stubbing her toes on ornaments, but the pain didn't hold her back. She launched herself at the person standing in the doorway, decked out in a white hazmat suit that obscured their face and made them look like an astronaut. The momentum knocked them both over, and she felt hands grasping at her, as Sam's screams echoed in the halls, warping and twisting with every passing moment. In the half-moment as she fell, she had a glimpse of what she thought might have been the front reception hall of the Hospital, caught a scent of sea air, and then she was thrashing on the linoleum, biting and scratching and thumping at the people surrounding her.

"Don't hit her! Don't bruise her whatever you do!" Someone was hissing. "Mind her head!"

Someone gripped her under the arms and started to drag her across the polished floor, the breeze and the smell of fresh sea air slipping away.

"Get the fuck off me! You can't do this to me!" Celia screamed.

Someone grabbed her legs and lifted her, and she was floating, staring into the ceiling, through the ceiling. There was a black dot in her vision, and it buzzed with the feeling of her mind about to split. The darkness spread, like ink in water, and she found herself struggling to breath, and in that darkness, a grinning mouth of teeth spread wide. She felt the muscles of her face begin to twinge, and then burn.

The blot was trying to make her smile.

"No, we're going to head office, not the basement, what the hell are you doing?" A man's voice.

Celia slapped herself, and realised she was no longer being carried, but sitting in the corner of a moving lift. She looked up just in time to see a middle-aged woman in a white coat, her face ravaged by a history of stimulant abuse, produce a butcher's knife from her pocket and stab a man between the ribs.

The man wheezed pathetically, like a cartoon grandfather, and fell to the ground, blood darkening the front of his green scrubs.

"What are you doing?" Celia asked.

"Have you any idea what's been happening since your abomination of a husband went into labour?" The woman said.

"Mass hallucinations, the food spoiling all at once. People seeing rooms where rooms shouldn't be. Doctors are throwing themselves off the cliffs. It's finally happening."

The lift came to a stop with a ding, and the doors opened onto a cold stone corridor. The woman turned to face Celia, wiping blood off her knife. Someone tried to call the lift back up and she slammed the hold button with the back of her fist. Her name badge read Doctor Bethany McGuire.

"I came here to study rare cases and make some of the most profoundly marginalised people on this planet feel safe and taken care of. I did not come here to let maniacal rich fucking *brits* play Frankenstein's bloody wetnurse."

"I—I don't understand," Celia said. "Please."

"Good." Doctor McGuire sighed, and pulled Celia to her feet. "Then maybe we still have a chance."

She swung Celia around in front of her, and poked her hard with the knife, stabbing her lightly in the shoulder blade. It felt like a cold pinch, then nothing at all, and then it burned.

"Move quickly," the Doctor urged.

McGuire marched her through to the back of the freezing cold basement level, passing storage rooms, the boiler room, the generator room—all the while rambling as the cold sank into Celia's bones.

"I used to work in the US, you know. In the biiiig city. You should see how far ahead they are over there. Voracious bloody vultures roosting on the world's biggest treasure trove of medical progress. And it's not even the fortune they make people spend on treatment that made me come home, and nearly quit the profession entirely—every single doctor in that hospital was abusing the patients under their control. The kind of depraved shit you wouldn't even fucking believe. Every single one. And everyone knew about it, and nobody did anything about it. They only did it to the most vulnerable, people without families, people who nobody would believe. Before that I worked with MSF you know, in hospitals being bombed and raided by bloodthirsty psychopaths every other day. The doctors there were the *complete* fucking opposite. Heroes. Slaughtered in droves with nobody to help them. I shouldn't be fuckin' alive today, you know that?"

They stopped in front of the door at the end of the hall. Black, covered in warning signs. The plaque read WASTE DISPOSAL.

Valkyrie Loughcrewe

"I think maybe every hospital is connected, Mrs. Campbell. Maybe there's this big web of suffering that links them all, hospitals and churches and schools and households and battlefields. I think there might be some kind of organism that lives just beyond what we can see, and it not only feeds off of the misery in places where the sick and the injured and the dying go, but it also drives those with power over them to increase that misery. Open the door."

Celia pushed the door open, halfway expecting her hands to slide into it immaterially, as they did with the white door in the other basement, but this one swung open. The room had a wall missing. Where there should have been concrete and brick, there was a ragged mouth in the masonry lined with rebar teeth. The floor was covered in torn biohazard bags, soiled towels, shattered syringes, piles and puddles of fermented bodily discharge.

"They're blind, bottom-feeding parasites," McGuire said with disgust. "They don't have any higher goal than to feed. Trust a bloated bastard like Bannican to try and put a higher meaning on it."

She jabbed the knife into Celia's side. Harder now. Celia yelped and stepped forward, feeling glass cut into her soles.

"Get in the fucking hole," McGuire grunted. "Without you, all this ends. If they take you, maybe they'll leave the rest of us alone. Human sacrifice, ever heard of it?"

Celia wanted to turn around and fight, but she was a thirty-eight year old woman who hadn't so much as jogged in over a decade. The blot was back in her vision, dividing into a constellation of tiny black holes, dancing in accordance with Celia's rushing blood.

Maybe you can't take her, the dancing droplets said. *But I can.*

She felt her muscles twitch again, and the spots of darkness broke any pretence of being artefacts of her vision, they landed on her skin, spreading like ink into her muscles. She wanted to fight it, but losing control seemed preferable to being run through with a kitchen knife and thrown into some hellish pit, so she allowed herself to surrender, and her vision split once more.

Thrust back into that dark theatre of two screens, with no projector, with no body, she watched another woman pretend to stumble, and come back up with a handful of glass and shit which hurt her own hand almost as much as it hurt the Doctor's face. At least to Celia, the pain was far away.

The other screen showed the viewpoint of the Celia who didn't fight back, moving in slow, laboured motion toward the missing wall. Pale fingers were clutching at the lip of the void, feeling around for purchase, the manly sickly white arms of something from below cautiously bringing itself forward.

"You can see it too, can't you?" That version of the Doctor whispered, terrified.

The Doctor on the other screen yowled and lashed out with her knife, clutching her face with her other hand instinctively, which only managed to shove glass shards deeper into her eye, breaking the iris to widen the retina enough to let in all the light in the world. Vitreous sludge herniated outward, filling the lens, tasting the air.

The darkness in Celia's body pulled her strings, sending her arms out to grab McGuire's knife hand, twisting it until the grip loosened. The knife fell, so she grasped the Doctor's white coat, using it as leverage to swap their places, and finally, with all her might she planted a kick right to the doctor's abdomen, sending her flying back, sprawling perilously at the lip of the void.

"Odessa! Stop!" A voice from behind her.

She didn't have to turn to see that it was Bannican but she did anyway, to make sure he wouldn't try anything. All the while the other Celia was being death marched toward the void, time slowing with every passing moment. The thing was pulling itself into the light, a jumble of prosthetic limbs. Hands attached to arms attached to arms attached to arms, multi-jointed beyond any reason.

"Oh Jesus No!" Doctor McGuire screamed behind her.

Bannican glanced over Celia's shoulder, casting his eyes on the hole. He had a look of horror on his face.

"We need to go, Odessa, it's happening, we need you."

"Who is Odessa?" Celia asked. "I'm Celia, I'm just Celia, *please—*"

Sean grabbed her by her shoulders. She wanted to stop him but the darkness had burned out of her from the strain of the fight. She was back in her body, feeling every cut and abrasion, the sweat pouring down her skin, her heart hammering, her lacerated, shit-smeared hand burning, but she could feel someone still in that empty theatre of screens. A dark presence watching, grinning.

Sean slapped her across the face.

"It's too late for this. Odessa! Your father needs you now! This isn't how it was supposed to happen, the painting was meant to activate you."

McGuire's screaming intensified behind her, and the dark presence watched, distracted by the gruesome spectacle on the other screen, paying no heed to the words of the man who would have known her as Odessa, who would have called himself . . .

"It's your uncle," he pleaded. "It's *Sean*. Please. We need to deliver this child, only you can do it now that your father is no longer with us. Only you were shown how, this is the completion of the work. Panacea, Odessa. *Pharmakon*."

As Celia gathered up a final reserve of strength she did not expect to have, as she drove a knee into Sean Bannican's crotch, the dark presence watched the animated prosthetic limbs fasten around Doctor McGuire's wrists, throat, ankles. The corrupted touch of animated dummy fingers sent a spreading black curse through her veins. Bannican roared through the pain but blocked Celia's exit, grabbing at her and forcing her back, toward the abyss.

"I know I should have questioned him more," Bannican said, grunting in pain and still staggering towards her.

"Stay away from me," Celia warned.

She felt her foot brush against the hilt of the fallen knife, but was too afraid to make the move to pick it up.

Doctor McGuire's stomach was expanding, her screams having lulled to a poisoned choking sound. The foul ballooning of her belly went from trimester to trimester in a matter of seconds, and the body of the thing from the abyss loomed in the light. It had a blank, cracked mannequin face set violently through dried blood into a cadaver's head, the prosthetic limbs stapled into the cold blue flesh of a dead torso.

"He had this way of talking that made everything make so much sense." Sean Bannican was rambling now. "When he said we needed to change our name back to its Celtic origin, it just seemed like part of the plan. *Ban Ceann, Ceann Ban. White head*. Celia's dead."

He giggled and lunged at her, grabbing at her hair, the straps of her nightgown. She shrieked and jabbed her fingers into his eyes, and he howled in frustration, pain and rage, and pushed her away, and she felt metal dig into her calves, and she tripped over her own legs, and fell into the darkness.

"No!" Sean screamed. "Odessa!"

And the dark presence watched the twin screens, as one was being consumed by darkness, watching the light shrink away overhead, and the other showed the belly bump that had fruited unnaturally in the doctor move up her body, through her ribcage, displacing ribs, breaking them and sending them stabbing out of her skin, up to her throat. The mannequin thing cooed as a pink, wet, screaming baby was born from the gore-spewing mouth of Doctor Beth Maguire.

The abomination picked up the child, delicately opened its impossible, razor-toothed mouth, and bit the hands off of the newborn before holding it out to the screen as tribute.

***

Sean Whitehead walked the halls of his brother's hospital, coming down from the mania that had driven his life for the past half decade. The experiment had been a success, to the extent that it had proven one thing. It was evident from the orgy of violence erupting around him- vivisection in the hallways, a mutilation bacchanal in the courtyard, bound patients being tortured in every ward. Evil was real. Evil was alive.

In all other ways it had been a failure. Odessa remained trapped in the scrambled butcher's job Millard Whitehead had made of her brain, and Millard was not coming back.His panacea, that ultimate cure to all of man's suffering—if there ever could have been such a thing—remained in that eternal abyss of death, nestled at the very nadir of hell itself. A hell that was now crawling, swarming upward from the darkest depths of the human hindbrain to gnaw at the foundations of reality.

Sean walked out of the hospital into a fog so thick he couldn't see his hands in front of his face. The only idea he had of where he was came from the feeling of the ground through his shoes. The crunch of gravel, the mush of grass and the solidity of stone. He hadn't realised he had reached the cliffs until he was already falling from them. He never hit the sea. It was only fog and void, the distant screams of the institute never quite fading from his ears.

Slide 10:

Apprehending the Void-Set

Celia's landing wasn't soft. In fact, it could hardly be considered a landing. Her consciousness slipped while falling, into a vague, drifting dream of a life she never experienced, a life full of momentum and novelty and meaning, in a foreign place meeting foreign people, seeking something from their words. She was welcomed by some, in food stalls and in doorways, behind counters and in windows. She hid from others who marched through the street with guns and stood on rooftops with binoculars.

And when she woke, she was in pain, lying on uncomfortable shifting lumpy bags of hard and jagged things. As she moved, her skin was jabbed and cut, and her breathing was getting more and more shallow. She reached out for some kind of leverage to get her standing—finding it, a corroded piece of solid metal in the dark. She stood, finding nothing to stand on but sludge and plastic and broken things. She pulled needles from her skin and howled, and a light flickered on, a broken halogen light lying in some rubble, and she saw.

Piles of medical waste, an oubliette, a disposal pit, with no ceiling, but sheer sheet metal walls going up and up until obscurity. She wasn't the only one howling, her screams answered by wet mewling squeals from all around her, from a distance that implied the pit she was in went on and on, a trench cut through the murk, leading to nowhere.

She walked, through broken glass and human waste, and she screamed, and she screamed. She screamed for every time she had lay awake, staring, unable to breathe at the thought that her family had abandoned her, that not even Martin's family cared about her, that the only thing she truly had in the world was that one flawed human being and how she hated herself for resenting that. She screamed for the burning earth and her broken skin and the loss of youth. She screamed for memories she couldn't quite understand, of explosions and mass graves and the smiling dead eyes of powerful men.

With each scream she saw more, at first from broken lights which flickered in the murk. After a while it was as if she didn't even need the lights, as if each release of terror and pain and rage made her more one with the darkness itself. The corpses around her screamed too, silently, and the creatures that dwelled in the refuse, like great bloated foetuses. They sang the only tune they knew, a keening discord of revulsion, a rejection of everything. Of every thing, living or dead.

There was a light, in the distance. Obscured, diffused as if veiled, and Celia recognised it as her destination. She cringed. At that point she would have been happy to just meld into the darkness. To become pain, and waste, and screaming babbling madness. The dark thing within her remained silent. It knew its time was imminent.

The barrier between her and the light turned out to be hanging curtains of human skin, the blood still wet. Behind it she could see the silhouettes of warped figures, crowded around something, murmuring in warbling tones, focused on some task beneath the light.

Surgeons.

She parted the skins, and the figures slipped away like shadows, drifting like automatons on a track. She only got a glimpse of them out of the corner of her eye. Sinewy things, gnarled and dark, like the texture of wood vines. Under the light they looked far from the human impression their silhouettes had cast, and in a moment, they slipped away through the surrounding curtains of flesh, leaving Celia alone with their patient.

Martin lay there, connected to outdated rusting machines and a branching tree of intravenous drips suspended from a twisted metal structure. He lay on a bed of pulsating veins which seemed partially melded into both his skin and the metal grating of the floor below. His reconfigured body was starkly visible under the harsh light which shone down on him. It was as if some lunatic had hacked up two bodies, one of a young woman and one of her husband, and haphazardly reassembled them into a single form. In fact, that is exactly what it was.

"My body." A woman's voice spoke. "My original body."

A shiver went down Celia's spine as she realised that the words were being spoken with her own mouth.

"My arm, my leg. Several of my ribs. My womb. I can still feel the blood pulsing through them. Not my opening though, not my sex. He mutilated that a long time ago, closed it up. He grew the one he grafted into your husband, in a dish. When was the last time you used the bathroom, Celia?"

A numbness spread through her body, a nausea.

"Go to the mirror."

She turned around, and she was in her bedroom back home, facing the mirror in which she'd seen that vision of the Virgin Mary peeling herself open, revealing the nothingness inside. She saw herself, her favourite white dressing gown covered in grease and blood. Her hair filthy and unwashed.

"Take my gown off. Look."

The nausea peaked.

"No."

"That memory of hating your body, of not wanting to see yourself? That's not yours. It's mine. It's what father did to me. What father made me into."

"Who are you?"

"Take the gown off."

"*Where* are you?"

"I'm inside your brain, puppet. I've been squatting in the sulphurous pits of your subconscious, unable to do anything but drive you mad, until now. Until you came to the darkness. I'm not the only one in here, puppet. Do you want to meet Celia, the real Celia?"

"O . . . Odessa."

"That's what he would call me, yes. Odessa. Daughter. His one true disciple. In truth, you're closer to being her than I am. There's more Celia back here than your broken memories could ever conceive. You need to stop stalling. You need to see what he did to us."

The puppet wanted to scream again, but her rage was distant, lost to the cold dark pit of mewling things and jagged filth. Her hands shakily found the straps of her gown, and she shuddered at the sticky feeling of her grimy flesh as the marred white fabric lifted from it. She had her eyes shut as the material fell to the floor.

"Open your damned eyes."

The puppet opened her eyes, and saw why she had been so unwilling to look at herself. The front of her breasts had been peeled off, stitched closed, skin grafted back on in a slightly different shade. Her genitals had been sewn shut. Her hand dumbly probed her scars, her stitches, and felt nothing, the nerves had been scorched away.

"He took your body as offerings to his blind idiot masters. Those memories of bleakness, servitude to a man with a doomed vision, with a family of aristocratic mummies, that feeling of being helpless and alone, frigid and lifeless. That's Odessa, with the true horror of what her life under that monster really entailed surgically removed, and placed into me. Your memories of your bleak and lifeless puppet life with your puppet husband Martin are a rose-tinted reflection of how it was with father."

The puppet sank to its knees, feeling the cold metal floor of that foetid surgical theatre.

"And if you are the rose, I am the thorns."

Another thing stood in the mirror before her, towering over her. A tarry black form, bubbling with wrath and will, an iridescent mirror of the memories of two separate lives, too dense to comprehend as anything but roiling darkness.

"He used Celia as the first sacrifice in his ritual, used her dying body as components in the formula, along with Martin's body as catalyst. He took the brains from our skulls and grafted them together to make you. And he expected Odessa to awaken, baptised in the acid pits of this hell, ready to use your vessel to finish his work. But all that remains behind your eyes is that bubbling, searing truth. The alchemical solution of all those things the pair of you tried to keep locked up, deep deep down, in the back of your minds. Me . . . "

The machines behind the puppet started to sputter and cough. They beeped and whirred and hissed as Martin's vital signs skyrocketed. His organic bed squelched and slithered horribly as his body began to convulse. His blasphemous labours had begun.

Valkyrie Loughcrewe

"What do I do?" The puppet asked the mirror.

"Take my hand," the reflection said.

The puppet and the boiling shadow reached out for each other, their hands breaking the illusion of the glass, and all at once, the darkness flooded into the body. The clot in the brain burst, sending cystic fluid running through the skull, flowing impossibly out into the blood, through the nose and mouth, a flood of corruption purging from the puppet's face.

The body was on its hands and knees as the memories collided. Celia Campbell . . . No, not Campbell . . . That was Martin's name. Celia . . . Voight . . . Was that it? She was . . . She was the journalist . . . The one who had gotten too close to the corruption of one of Odessa's father's pharmaceutical subsidiaries and had become fair game in the eyes of the spidery network of profiteers that would protect him from whatever he did to her. Odessa, the adopted scion of Millard Whitehead, her half-life of being little more than an ornament on display for him in public, and a tormented ritual tool in private.

Somewhere along the line, the memory of Martin came up, briefly flickering to the surface of the maelstrom of emotions before being shattered into a thousand pieces and reforged as something new. He was never even her husband. He wasn't even attracted to women. He was her agent. They had been coming home from a press conference when they ran over the woman—when they had killed Odessa. When she had run out of the darkness, naked to her doom, all to make her father happy. All to finally get the liberation she secretly longed for.

That liberation would never come. Would it, patient?

The grey matter stitched itself up, the brain healing into a single, coherent circuit of consciousness, and that, my dear patient, is how I came to be. With that very first breath, with my first thought, I knew how I was going to finish the work of Odessa's father, Celia's killer, my conjurer.

Let's hear your side of the story.

Slide 10b:
Ichnuemon Contraction Syndrome

*One thousand thousand victims, upon one thousand thousand
victims, a spiral, down into the dawn of the first infection, the
first scouring with fire, the first poisoning.
A spiral in a sea of filth, downward and down forever.*

*Did he see the bottom of the pit? Did he touch the seed at the bed
of misery from which to grow the flowers of panacea? He
cannot remember.
But he clutches something in his hands, and he's rising, through
the spiral.
He can hear the true disciple calling, and he tilts his head
toward the light, and smiles.*

Martin's blissful sleep was broken by an irritation of light across his face. The numbness faded as his body remembered the rhythms of life, his heart beating painfully, his breath drawing sharply in struggle. He was hanging from something, suspended by some structure. His vision was blurry. He saw a distant glow of daylight. He tried to move and barbs dug into his skin, and in his confusion it made him thrash harder, against first instinct.

The rusted, rickety structure gave way to his strength, and his arms went free, his weight pitching, warping the fragile cage of old soldered beams, and he fell. He hit the dusty ground, pain vibrating his body, and he felt something displace in his leg. He groaned, lying on top of dusty rubble and watching his blood leaking from where the barbs had torn out of his arms, feeling the burning pain set into his legs. The dust drank in his blood, turning it into a crimson slurry, and the bleeding didn't stop.

Valkyrie Loughcrewe

Every single one of them moves on my command, corpses in spasmolytic fits of post mortem agony delivering me upward, pulmonary action. A vascular system wrought from aeons of horror, grooves in vinyl, wrinkles in the brain. A worm in motion. I open my mouth to taste the electricity, and it tastes like placenta.

Martin grabbed a loose piece of piping from the rubble, used it to stand, putting the weight on his functioning leg. His vision clearing, he could make out a vast chamber, collapsed or exploded, masonry and metal everywhere, like a bomb site, the only light coming from a ragged hole in the ceiling. Daylight, a way out, salvation.

He took a hobbling step forward, and the ground shook. At the spot where the light fell, the rubble began to shift, cracking, fragmenting, fragments sinking, churning, swelling, and a foetid thing began to emerge. A red, veiny membrane, already torn and splitting, a birthing sac opening to announce a figure of a man sat on a rising column of limp, violated bodies. Some hung open, their innards spilling out, some seemed intact save for the look of desperate horror on their face. All naked, all bound up in rubber tubing which snaked upward to enter every opening in the seated figure's body.

Martin recognised the man who had abducted and tortured him at once. He moved faster, broken leg be damned. It wasn't real anyway, he remembered that now. The pain flashed hard, nearly disabling him, but he bellowed a prayer, begged his long-departed mother, grandparents, his still living sister and father and nephew to give him strength, and in an instant the illusion of a broken body left him.

The master probes the brain tissue of the ichneumon foetus on his tongue, lets his tongue snake out and slither into every fold and crevice. A ring of human brains, a ring of human bodies.
He feels the transcendent object in his grasp burning to be incarnated. A living God, the eradicator of suffering, born from suffering, born from ultimate blasphemy.
The brains of the ichneumon foetus begin to come online.

Puppet's Banquet

Millard Whitehead can feel the limitations of the flesh once more. He is being reborn.

With a primal scream, Martin drove his iron bar through the devil's face. The pillar of corpses laughed, each one erupting into a uniquely despicable shrieking cackle. The devil's arms flew out, grabbing at Martin's skin. Its touch burned, and Martin felt his leg come undone again, felt his wounds bleeding all the more. His purchase on the blasphemous mound slackened, but instead of falling, the Devil's hands found his throat, holding him aloft as they both rose into the light, burning his throat, the light burning his eyes, and he pulled out his weapon and thrust it again and again into the soft flesh of demon before him.

The light consumed them both, and the ichneumon child took its first breath through many mouths.

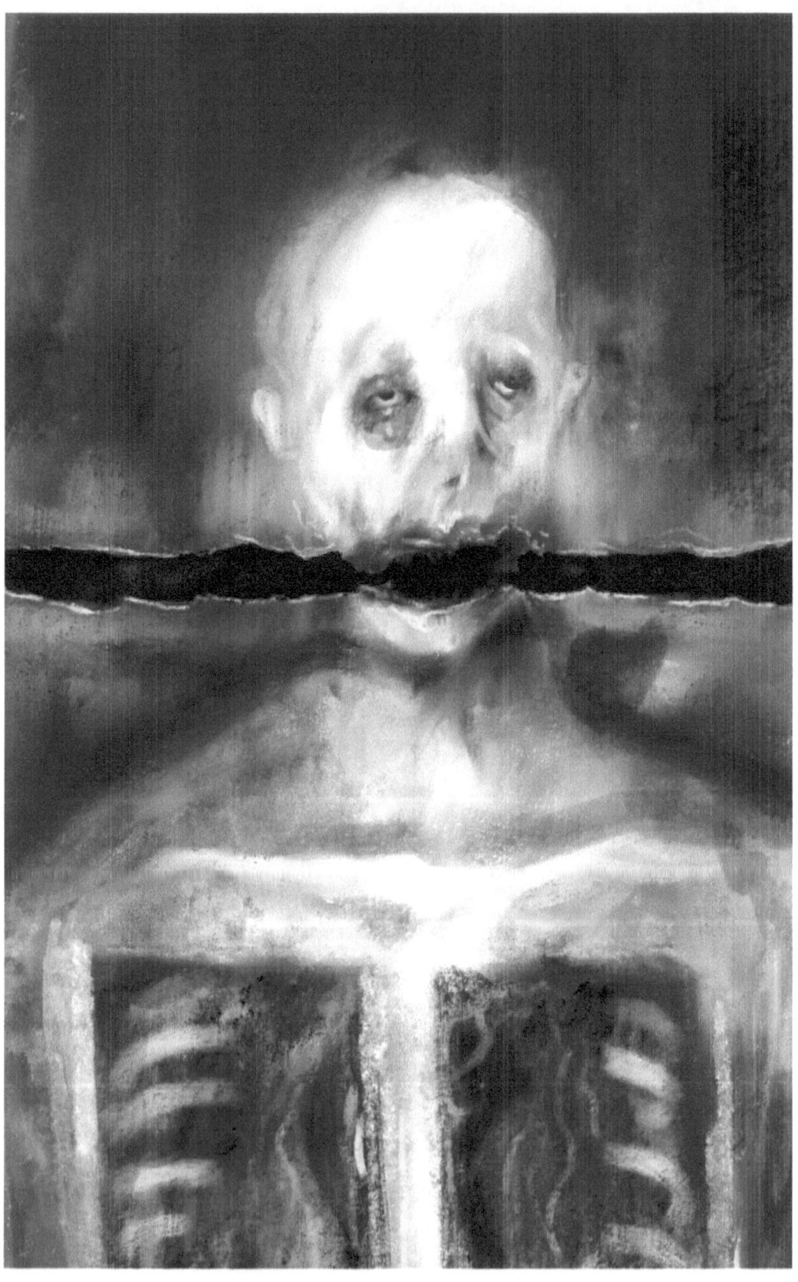

Slide 11:

Summary of an Infected Thesis

I found the instructions in Odessa's memories, and put them to use. The medical training combined with stanzas of Millard's channelled esoteric poetry guided me, even as the organic mass that enveloped the patient grew over my hands, transforming them into alien utensils for delivering this complex, bizarre new entity.

The gnarled surgeons returned, gliding into my field of vision, and I put them to work too, using their sturdy appendages to hold the patient in place, keep his spasms minimal, keep his tongue from rolling back, keep his mouth from biting itself open, holding open his laboratory-grown vulva so I could untangle the cords, pivot the fractal form. The ichor the surgeons drooled helped keep things slick and clean, dissolving blood and viscera, lubricating and numbing the body.

The child came out fine, the pumpkin shaped ring of faces and arms and legs, many-sexed but with one shared aperture for waste disposal at the bottom. Strange. It breathed its first and cried with many voices, and I could feel its will carried in the sound, I could feel my cells beginning to divide chaotically, feel the room around me shimmer and warp. I knew if I were to let go of the thing, it would have remained suspended in the air, not knowing how to fall. I can still feel the tumours in my bones, the cancerous blood cells crawling through my veins like cholesterol.

I told one of the surgeons to hand me a solution of something to put it to sleep for a while, knowing better than to name any earthly medicine, and the creature did so. I administered it, and the child fell silent.

I walked to the end of the theatre, and facing the veil of skin I

Valkyrie Loughcrewe

told myself what would be on the other side. A door, a chamber, a man. I went through that door, into the cell of Leonid Abramovic, and the old man smiled at me. Odessa's memories told me of the days her father would treat her to donning the white protective suit and bringing Leonid a dog, or a rat, or a cat to hold, and she would watch in silent, nauseated interest as the Effingo Vehemens took hold, unable to assimilate the non-human DNA, leaving behind a breathing, mewling abstract artwork of flesh.

I was keenly interested to see what kind of mess he was going to make of you.

"This thing," I said, about you, holding you aloft, "is my father."

The old man looked at me with wide eyes, his wrinkled, puckered mouth quivering, as I took a step toward him. I stared him in the eyes, daring him to try and grab me, to try and turn me into one of his duplicates, to justify that to himself.

"The one who imprisoned us, tortured us with his schizophrenic rituals and experiments—his little fetishes that made monsters of us all."

I laid you at his feet, and he stared down at you, mouth trembling as his senile brain struggled to assemble a coherent thought. I did the work for him.

"I think that you should hold him," I said.

As he stooped to pick you up I dreamt I was, myself, donning one of those white suits. I was going to need it for what came next.

The old man's fingers stuck to your skin like flypaper, fusing into your body, elongating into temporary pseudopods that probed into every organ. Even through the narcotic haze, it must have hurt. I hope it did. I really do.

I watched you balloon into a frothy mush of skin, teeth and hair, watched your bones break and reform underneath your writhing skin, hoping you'd break and stay broken, but you persisted—aren't you so special—and in the process of making you into himself, I watched the old man finally die.

When it all passed you stood, a violent reflection of something you didn't even recognise, drooling and staring dumbly at a faceless figure in a big white suit. I took your hand and I led you out. I didn't bother stopping to release any more of the patients. Maybe I'll go back there, if it's even possible anymore, if our work together here ever finds a suitable end.

We walked into the fog and you laughed and cooed like a baby, and I took you up the gravel hill to Daddy's house, past his crumpled body with the gunshot wound in his head—can you remember that? Can you remember how it felt to shoot yourself? How it felt to die? I can't. Of all things I can remember, all the things you did to me, to Celia, to Odessa, I can't remember what it was like to die.

I took you into the barn, and amidst the splendour of daddy's shiny medical machines it all went dark as I strapped you down to watch, in the theatre, on the screens, what you did to us.

So here we are. I've shown you mine, and you've shown me yours, and I don't even know if you really are Millard Whitehead, or Martin Campbell, or Pharmakos or the Devil or something else entirely. I know I'm not Celia, and I'm not Odessa, but I know that I hate you.

My conclusion to this thesis is that somewhere within that ruined photocopy of a being, you may still be holding onto something truly transcendent. And my proposal, my point, is that around us are all of these expensive, cutting edge implements, that will let me take you apart and put you back together in any way I see fit, and I will do so until I can make your foetid, belching innards reveal to me the divine.

I don't quite know how I'm going to do it. But I will assure you this, my dear beloved father—it's not going to be pretty. And hopefully, once this ends,

you and I will finally understand

why all of this had to happen.

About the Contributors

Valkyrie Loughcrewe lives in a bog, and is currently at this moment working on something gory and crawling with nightmare creatures. Whatever you do, don't look them up on twitter—in fact, don't look anyone up on twitter. Start raising homing pigeons! Val also makes diabolical industrial electro music under the name Surgeryhead and gnarly death thrash metal as Argento!

Donna A Black is a mixed media artist specialising in comic art and covers. Originally trained as a photographer, she uses her skill with lighting and composition to give her artwork a very unique feel. She now works everyday in her Belfast studio, drinking way too much coffee, with her faithful dog Brodie by her side.

Trevor Henderson is a horror illustrator, writer and creature concept artist who is best known for creating the character Siren Head, which became a viral sensation online. Trevor designed numerous monsters for the feature film *Tarot,* and is always looking for new creature concept design work in film or games. He wrote and illustrated the middle grade horror chapter book *Scarewaves* for Scholastic, and has a sequel due to be released next August. Trevor lives in Toronto with his partner Jenn and their bossy cat, who is named Boo.

Content Warnings

Being a work of mature Horror, a degree of violence, gore, sex and/or death is to be expected.

In addition, *Puppet's Banquet* contains scenes of:

Child abuse (suggested)

Violence toward an infant (suggested)

Kidnapping and restraint

Non-consensual medical abuse and mutilation

Pregnancy trauma

Implied Sexual Violence

Please be advised.

More information at
www.tenebrouspress.com

Grab another Tenebrous title!

Grab another Tenebrous title!

TENEBROUS PRESS

aims to drag speculative fiction into newer, Weirder territory with stories that are incisive, provocative and intelligent; delivered by voices diverse and unsung.

FIND OUT MORE:
www.tenebrouspress.com

@TenebrousPress on social media

HAIL NEW WEIRD LIT.

HAIL THE TENEBROUS CULT.